THE BOY OF THE ORANGES

THE BOY OF THE ORANGES

Author: Giulia Poli Disanto
Copy Editor: Tiziano Thomas Dossena
Editor: Leonardo Campanile
Cover Design & Interior Layout: Dominic A. Campanile

Translation by Tiziano Thomas Dossena of the original novel
"Il Ragazzo delle arance" by Giulia Poli Disanto.

ISBN: ISBN: 978-1-948651-71-4
Library of Congress Control Number: 2025942855
Published by: Idea Press *(an imprint of Idea Graphics, LLC)* — Florida, USA
www.ideapress-usa.com • www.lideamagazine.com
Administrative Office, Florida, USA • email: ideapress33@gmail.com
Editorial Office, New York, USA • editoreusa@gmail.com

Printed in the USA - 1st Edition, July 25, 2025

GIULIA POLI DISANTO

- TRANSLATED BY TIZIANO THOMAS DOSSENA -

THE BOY OF THE ORANGES

"... For years we look for small things in the infinite universe...

and then, suddenly, we find the infinite universe in a

small little world."

Anonymous

To Mario and my nephews Antonio and Francesco, Light of my eyes

To my parents, from whom I inherited the love for writing

Acknowledgements

All writers, from time to time, see their lives reflected in the pages they write. I, too, don't deny it; I haven't strayed much from a reality hinted at by events that, for better or worse, my son has woven into each day. And at the end of the journey, there's always a way to say thank you:

To Mario, for the good days.

To Marilena, for the constancy with which she diligently recorded dialogues with my son in a diary, over the years, as reported by me in the novel.

To the legendary Marilù, Spanish by origin, for having tried to teach Mario the clock, with the result that he ended up preferring even numbers.

To Vitogiulio, for having initiated him into the study of the calendar.

To the unsurpassed teacher Giacomina, for all the times she managed to orient him in the reality of life with games, nursery rhymes, thoughts, simple recipes, and much more.

To Franco, for his visits home when Mario was depressed.

To the many families, for the dignity and composure with which they face the handicap.

And then:

To Gabriella Genisi, for lending me Commissioner Lolita Lobosco.

To Mary; she knows why.

To the school and to my students, dispassionately, even though for some years I have set aside the role of a teacher to embrace, full-time, that of an author.

I

To my colleagues, for their willingness to make my writings reading journeys.

I can't overlook...

Angela Giannelli, for her enthusiasm and beautiful words of encouragement.

Giulia Notarangelo, for her tasty review of my **Cherries at midnight**—diary of a thirteen-year-old girl—Negroamaro ed. 2012, of which I reported excerpts in the chapter "But my mother likes detective stories."

A ring that was stolen from me.

The turtles that, in summer, prove to be sweet company.

My sisters Maria Grazia and Giovanna, for having played an important role in Mario's life.

My mother, for her tenacity, despite her ninety-nine years.

My husband, my children, my whole family, who, in some way, have contributed to the writing and growth of this *FUNTHRILLER* and who continually ask me: *"When is the next book?"* I don't know if they will like this story, but I loved writing it.

All readers who will have the patience to share this adventure with me.

Introduction

by the Author

"The word autistic is frightening," says journalist Gianluca Nicoletti, *"it embodies the mystery of madness, of which he does not bear the outward signs. A moral prejudice also weighs on this disease: it is believed that children become autistic because of their mothers, who have 'done something wrong'."*

Before my third child was born, I knew nothing about autism. It was when he turned two that I noticed some unusual behaviors in him that were identified as autistic. The traits of Asperger's syndrome emerged after a complicated surgery at four months old, following a right temporal abscess, which resulted in a brain injury.

During my research, I learned that autism is a phenomenon (whose origin is unknown) that generally manifests in the early years of a child's life and could also result from encephalitis or a brain lesion that compromises the normal neurological development process. The latter coincided with my son's problem.

Although there is a significant intellectual deficit, these children are not limited; instead, they are very intelligent, even though they use a unique and repetitive language known as echolalia.

The difficulty in speaking (which is rather subjective) and interacting with people is just one of the hallmarks of these subjects who, due to their inability to communicate, assume behaviors of dissociation from the reality in which they live. They behave as if they were deaf and avoid all physical and visual contact, thus favoring their isolation, which may last a lifetime. Repetitive body movements or self-stimulating behaviors such as clapping hands, rocking, and spitting are quite common.

Autistic individuals often struggle with playing interactive games, sharing emotions, forming friendships, and understanding the thoughts and feelings of others. They may display inappropriate and stereotyped gestures, feeling like prisoners of their own personality. Changes or unexpected occurrences are seen as threats and can trigger intense anger, leading to self-harming behaviors such as hitting their heads with fists, pulling their hair, or damaging their nails. An obsessive attachment to unusual objects (such as strings, strips of paper soaked in saliva, and various knick-knacks) represents another aspect of the challenge. The degree of disability varies from individual to individual, and their daily experiences depend significantly on the people around them.

The protagonist of this FUNTHRLLER, a neologism that I coined where Fun stands for Funny / Different, is undoubtedly among those individuals endowed with enormous receptivity and exceptional memory. Tobia's "Story" aims to explore this challenging universe and highlight the uniqueness and complexity of relationships with individuals on the autism spectrum.

Any analogy involving facts, places, and people is completely coincidental.

INDEX

	— A Parrot and Mrs. Cristina	1
Chapter 2	— The Story of Tobia	5
	— Mrs. Cristina's Ring	11
Chapter 4	— Two Particular Carabinieri	15
	— When you are Sad, Sing!	19
Chapter 6	— My Mom, Just like the Phoenix	23
	— Holidays in Porretta Terme	27
Chapter 8	— I Hate Detective Stories	31
	— But My Mother Likes Detective Stories	35
Chapter 10	— Teacher Giacomina	39
	— My School	45
Chapter 12	— A Night Full of Nightmares	49
	— With my Friend, Pilù	53
Chapter 14	— Mala Tempora Currunt!	57
	— My Highlight	61
Chapter 16	— The Garden of Happy Children	65
	— Tommy	69
Chapter 18	— Madame Fantasy is a Fantasy	73
	— My Escape	77
Chapter 20	— Bari Station	81
	— Under the Starry Sky	85
Chapter 22	— The Boy of the Oranges	89
	— The Police Commissioner Lolita Lobosco, then Finally Home!	93

Chapter 24 — Back to School 99
— Archimedes' Principle 103
Chapter 26 — My Investigation 107
— Over Mrs. Cristina 111
Chapter 28 — The Button, The Body of Evidence 115
— The Odds of Extended Families 119
Chapter 30 — A Basketball Game 123
— A Mystery to be Solved 127
Chapter 32 — A Terrible Misunderstanding 133
— Four Brothers 137
Chapter 34 — Letters and Recipes 141

The Parrot
and Mrs. Cristina

I would never have written this story if Mrs. Cristina's parrot had not gotten her neck stuck in the iron bars of her cage. I met her every day on the road leading to my school; so much so that, in the long run, she became a companion in my games and conversations.

Mrs. Cristina's parrot was there that morning, too. Her neck was out of her prison, and she was flapping her wings like a hen about to be slaughtered.

It was clear that she was in trouble.

I opened the door. I had seen it done thousands of times by Mrs. Cristina. I freed her neck and placed her on the ground. The parrot stopped quivering and, as if she understood my good intentions, began to shake off her fear. Still stunned and using her wings as two wooden hangers, she dragged herself zigzagging across the asphalt, stopping only when she found herself in front of the tips of my shoes.

Zigzag is a word I always use; my teacher Giacomina taught it to me one day when we drew a series of transverse lines on the ground with yellow packing tape, joined together by many sharp angles. We walked on it for a whole week and had a lot of fun. We called the first transverse line that went up "zig," and the second line that went down "zag." Taken by euphoria, we drew many others, ultimately creating a strange staircase with steps that were sometimes uphill and sometimes downhill.

So, the parrot walked, zigzagging, looking at me with shining eyes that seemed almost out of their sockets, its pale-yellow beak open and its wings flapping like a pump at full speed.

She was a handsome specimen, as big as two fists put together, with a forked tongue that kept the whole neighborhood upside down.

"Zigzag! Zigzag!" repeated the animal, aiming the words at me. And not satisfied with her talking, she added: "Sooner or later I'll catch you, my lovebird! Sooner or later, I'll catch you, my lovebird!"

I looked around, but the only ones there at that moment were my friend Pilù and I.

Before I met Chicorita, I didn't know that animals could talk too. But Chicorita, as Mrs. Cristina called her, was a parrot, and I learned later that parrots are easily tamed. They learn to repeat words, the silliest phrases, songs, and, if you want, even swear words. They eat seeds and sometimes insects.

My friend Pier Luca, or Pilù as I call him, knows everything about parrots and claims that the female broods in the nest while the male provides the food.

Chicorita, in all likelihood, must have been a Polynesian or Australian female Loriidae because she had many colors and fed on vegetable juices; she did not brood and did not have a male to keep it company, but on the other hand, it said many swear words such as "*Piss Pot,* come forward, and idiot of a bird!"

I was born in Bari, but I live in Santeramo. Every village, as we know, has its own characteristics, and mine had Chicorita, the only parrot able to speak.

When I think of my town, I feel the wind blowing through my chest. The teacher, Giacomina, says that this feeling is called tenderness. So, she taught me that my city is located on a beautiful hill in the Murgia section of the Bari province, and I live in a neighborhood divided into two: one here and one there, with a large street in the middle. Between us, two is my favorite number, like all even numbers, so I decided that the chapters of this story, now that I know how to count better, will only be marked with even numbers.

On this side of the road, as I mentioned, there are many villas and employed individuals. However, beyond that, there are numerous public housing units occupied by people who are unemployed and who, to make a living, *tighten their belts*. I don't say this, but I have heard it from the adults who believe they always know everything. And "tightening the belt," I learned later, is just a way of describing the life of all those people who are in financial difficulty and do not say it.

My mother says there are two categories of people in the world: the rich, who enjoy a good time, and those who tighten their belts. Then, there are the poor devils, who seem as if they do not exist in the eyes of the world.

Mrs. Cristina and Chicorita actually belonged to the latter category and lived across the street. That morning, Pilù and I had been there for quite a while, playing with the animal after saving it from certain death, when we heard Mrs. Cristina shout: "Sooner or later, I'll catch you, you rascal!"

I had heard the same sentence pronounced by her parrot, and if the latter had not ended with two swear words such as "bastard, cuckold!" Mrs. Cristina would not have said anything new. It was a difficult situation, and I don't know how to behave in difficult situations, so I looked at her in amazement because I couldn't understand the reason for so much fuss.

While Pilù managed to escape, Mrs. Cristina ran toward me with her arms raised in the air. She grabbed my wrist and forcefully dragged me into the small garden, where roses, geraniums, freesias, and many other fragrant flowers grew. I, not being very fast, remained standing there.

I looked up and saw the lady in her dressing gown, my arm caught in her pale-yellow claws, similar to a parrot's beak. I had been her prisoner for several minutes when I heard her scream once more.

"Hey, devil of a petty thief, give me back my ring, or else, I swear, I'll report you to the police!"

My mother always tells me to be kind to others, even when they test my patience, so I didn't react.

My father, who holds a different opinion, sometimes repri-
mands her with an "Ah, Penelope, don't talk bullshit!"

Then, feeling lost, I placed my arm on her chest and pushed
her away, believing that was the only way to free myself. After that, I
crouched on the ground, removed my shoes, and began to scream and
spit while tearing up all the flowers in her garden. Finally, I lay on
the asphalt, staring at the clouds floating in the sky, resembling many
threatening drawings.

The Story of Tobia

− CHAPTER 2 −

When I was a child, everyone called me a whelp, but I didn't know what it meant. Now that I'm grown up, I'm Tobia, Tobia Barbato, and I'm the best boy in the world. I don't always have a clear perception of myself, but I know who I am. For example, I am a boy who gets excited and confused easily, expresses himself in the third person, and has finally learned what it means to be a whelp, which is a playful term for son.

For family and friends, however, I am the son of Penelope and Vittorio. Yet, when others speak about me, they refer to me as "Tobia the disabled." This disappoints me because it suggests that they have doubts about me. Every night, before falling asleep, I review my personal data in my mind so I don't forget it.

My mother says that no one can choose the color of their skin. I was born with white skin, but it's merely a coincidence. Then there are children with yellow, pink, and chocolate skin; however, in our hearts, we are all the same.

When one is born, he is so young that he cannot give himself a name; this is why parents exist. Mom and Dad usually choose the names for their children. My parents called me Tobia, which in Hebrew is Tobijah and means "pleasing to the Lord."

That I am pleasing only to Him, does not surprise me.

My name, Tobia, consists of five letters, making it odd. However, sometimes I transform it into Toby, which also ends with a 'y', making it even. My brother Matthew says it sounds like the name of a big cat while he coughs, but I like it anyway. My surname also has an odd number of letters, but let's forget about that.

My friend Pier Luca's name, on the other hand, is even, but it remains a big problem for me because I never know whether to call him Pier or Luca. Only over time did I learn that Pier and Luca refer to the same person. To simplify things, I invented the name Pilù.

He's the only true friend I have. I find my other friends to be nerve-wracking because they don't want to play with me. Perhaps it's because sometimes I have panic attacks when suddenly I feel so many chicks coming into my head and running around, creating maddening confusion. Or maybe it's because, at other times, I see too little and feel a bit too much, unleashing great chaos within me that I cannot control. Or perhaps everything terrifies me, leaving me frozen in place until I gradually start to rock, spit, or clap my hands, with people staring at me as if I were an extraterrestrial, saying, "Maybe you have some problem..."

Then, my father intervenes:

"Hey, baby, stop! Otherwise, these pieces of shit get scared."

And I usually answer:

"Leave them be, because they are like Martians!"

My father is right, but people are still strange because they don't understand how I feel when I stammer or stutter, and I even get the accents wrong due to the thoughts that struggle to form. So, when I have difficulty finding the words necessary to create a decent conversation, I get clever and, feeling estranged from the world around me, methodically repeat all the words I hear, such as Tobia, get up – Tobia, have breakfast – Tobia, shut up!

It's just another method to defeat those stupid chicks that pop up in my head every time I feel anxious.

That's how my mind works. The neuropsychiatrist, who studies the nervous and mental systems and whom my father refers to as a shrink, explained to my parents that constantly repeating what you hear—an automatic repetition of words or phrases—is a neuropsychiatric disorder. For this reason, what I consider a specialty is referred to by experts as echolalic language.

If I had to guess, as my mother says, I deduce that even Mrs. Cristina's parrot has an echolalic language because it repeats everything that is said. However, my mother has explained to me many times that Chicorita is an animal, while I, thank God, am a boy (difficult to manage, but still a boy).

Well, I understand that this is the difference between the beast and the man. Another distinction, however, is that I go to school while Mrs. Cristina's parrot does not.

At school, I am fortunate to have teachers who are proud of me because, when I enter the classroom, I instantly register in my mind who is absent. This situation is convenient for them, as they can take advantage of it and avoid taking attendance.

I also get good grades in tests that assess memory, particularly when it comes to recalling the birthdays of everyone I know, the license plates of vehicles I see on the road, and all the important dates on the calendar. My father says that I am truly a genius in this field because I am unbeatable.

Let me provide an example: when someone wants to know which day corresponds to a specific date in a particular month, they ask me, "Tobia, can you please tell me the day that corresponds to June 20, 2000?" I activate my brain, which works like a computerized calendar; I push the button, input the information, and reply: "Tuesday." Or, "Tobia, what day of the week will June 20, 2024, be?" Using the same system, I simply respond: "Thursday."

I know all the songs from the Seventies and Eighties by heart. I'm also good at remembering the members of the World Cup soccer team and, at times, writing poems and other things that I can't recall at the moment.

I'm not sure if being afraid of wind and rain is a "problem," but when the weather is bad, I lock myself in the house and play with my collection of colored cars, which I often misplace, forcing my family to search for them and find them.

I also collect colored glass marbles and have a bag full of them. Since they have been forbidden to me for everyone's safety, I hide them under the mattress. When my mother makes the bed, I have a lot of fun as the marbles fall on the floor and scatter around the room. Then, she warns:

"Young man, how many times do I have to tell you not to place any marbles under the mattress? One day we'll step on them and break our necks!"

At least, my mother calls me a young man... but I pretend not to hear it and let myself slide on the floor. I pick up a handful and let them fall back, enchanted by their bounce, while she screams:

"Stop it, Tobia. I am fed up!", which, translated into everybody else's language, means: "Enough, Tobia. I can't take it anymore!"

Then I wander around the house, looking for small objects to enrich my collection. Just the other day, I found pencils, pens, erasers, a ticket for a concert in Bologna that belonged to my brother, and... my father's driver's license in a drawer.

My backpack is so full that it might burst someday.

Okay for the pens and pencils, but I won't reveal what happened when my brother and father desperately searched for the ticket and driver's license!

I also placed the sink cap in my bag. However, my mother, with her typical complaint, protested:

"Oh no, Tobia, what stress you cause... Give it to me, please!"

This is a game I can't resist, and the Shrink has called it by the strange name of kleptomania. When I told my friend Pilù, he replied not to worry because that's the name of a new medicine, if not a new cough syrup. So, I can't understand my father when he screams in my ears:

"By all the geese on Capitol Hill, baby, you may not understand, but those objects are not yours!"

But I swear I don't do it on purpose, even if my father calls me *baby*, and it inconveniences the geese of the Capitol.

Nevertheless, the best thing in my life happened when I was three years old.

My teacher Giacomina arrived one day with a smile on her lips and her shoulder bag. She seemed like an ordinary girl, easy to discourage, but I was mistaken. On the contrary, she was an intelligent, determined, and punctilious woman, and from the very first moment, she demonstrated her firm intention to win me over with patience and sweetness.

It took her three years to touch me and five years to make me speak—an amazing result, as I could finally be caressed and held in someone's arms without feeling excruciating pain (very similar to skinning) and could pronounce the first meaningful words. Slowly, I became attached to her.

She taught me that I had a father, a mother, and two older brothers: Hector and Matthew, specifying that my parents, in turn, had parents called grandparents. They also had brothers and sisters, whom I should have called uncles. Finally, I learned that there are also friends. Thanks to her, I learned that I am a male, like my father and my brothers, and that I am different from females because I have a wiener.

The only female in the house is my mother, and she has a cookie.

With the help of teacher Giacomina, I assembled this album titled "The Story of Tobia." After writing my story, I like to draw a parrot about the size of two fists at the bottom of each page.

So it was that when I met Chicorita, Mrs. Cristina's parrot, I called her "As big as two fists."

Besides all this, I don't understand what my "problem" entails.

Mrs. Cristina's Ring

My school is unlike any other.

As my father says, it is a school with a capital "S." And, if he says so, you must believe it. It is a school that makes no distinction between able-bodied and disabled children. This term, after all, is an elegant way to avoid saying handicapped, and I discovered that only by chance.

One day, I was in the lab with my electronics professor – a real stand-up guy, as my father defines him. He was discussing with another colleague the term "handicap" and other idioms, such as "disabled," "differently abled," or "on the autism spectrum," as they say lately. In my opinion, they are so many different words to express the same idea in an elegant way.

I, of course, did not intervene because I was not consulted.

I thought that even my uncle Tommaso, who uses a cane to walk, was no longer a handicapped person but rather a disabled person; or my literature teacher who, when she walks, drags her feet; or my mother's cousin who, being asthmatic, constantly takes inhalations; or my grandmother who, in order to live, must take insulin immediately after meals. In short, we are all differently abled in this world; the important thing is to recognize it.

Now, I finally know too.

Fortunately, I don't place much importance on this nonsense, and even if I can't relate well, I have many friends. For example,

I know Michael, who is in fifth grade and is always around the girls. And, as my mother says, he acts as a blundering fool with them.

Then there is Maria, who has a great piece of ass, is incredibly beautiful, and attends the same class as I do. I would gladly go out in her company because I have fallen so deeply in love with her. However, I don't know how to tell her, so I become mute. When I can, I hug her and hold on to her chest as long as possible because I enjoy feeling my heart lose its rhythm.

Then there is Xavier, who is always in the bathroom with a cigarette in his mouth. He is stuck up, and when someone wants to take a puff, he always says:

"Leave, as there is no tripe for cats here!"

There are still many other friends, but I am not going to describe them now, to avoid boring you.

However, I need to tell you something more about Pier Luca, even though I have already talked about him. He is a very cheerful guy, despite calling himself a loser. To capture my attention, he often tells jokes. He wears faded jeans with dirt stains all over them. On the left nostril of his nose, he wears a tiny fake diamond chip that resembles a mole born in the wrong place. His legs are long and thin, and he runs like a train.

The other day he told me that maybe he would stop coming to school because only donkeys go there. Well, it may be as he says, but if I have learned many things, it is thanks to school. However, he is somewhat right because it is not easy to repeat the same class for the third consecutive year. And I know something about that. According to what the professors say, I must improve my knowledge, while he needs to decide to study.

Pilù doesn't like to study; it's true. However, he knows everything about parrots. The literature teacher continues to tell him that knowing everything about parrots is not enough for promotion and suggests he should take a nice bath in the Holy Water to inspire a desire to study.

His house is not far from mine. He lives across the street, in those houses where you *tighten your belt*, and his family often tightens belts to make a living. My mom says that his mother died when he was born and that his father remarried soon after. So, when she tidies up my closet, she gives him my clothes. "Anyway," she says, "he's the same size as you. You look like twins!"

Pier Luca, however, never comes to my house because my father doesn't allow him. He says that where he has eyes, he also has hands. I don't understand. How can he have hands instead of eyes? So, I think that even my father, every now and then, shoots some big bullshit.

I usually meet my schoolmates near Mrs. Cristina's house because we have fun making her parrot talk. But Mrs. Cristina has been fed up with this for some time and threatens to report us to the carabinieri for disturbing the peace. When she gets angry, she points at us with her index finger, which is very long, tapered, and colored with fiery red nail polish, just like blood, showing off a very eye-catching ring on her ring finger.

Under the sun, that ring gives off a shimmer that escapes no one: it is certainly not a fake one. When I told my aunt, who knows about those things, she replied that it was certainly a *solitaire*.

Then, I thought that all people who live alone have a *solitaire* on their fingers. My aunt, on the other hand, explained to me that the ring had a precious stone called *a solitaire* and had nothing to do with her living alone. Good for her, I thought; evidently, she was not so poor a devil as my mother often said.

With the passage of time, Mrs. Cristina's house became our favorite place to meet. Her house was in a building with several floors, where she took care not only of cleaning but also of checking who came in or who left. Every morning, a swarm of boys who enjoyed making fun of her parrot gathered in front of it.

"What the fuck are you doing there!" shouted Pilù to the animal, when we passed her closely. In the end, I also began to make the same noise to him before running away to enter the classroom when lessons started. The parrot would repeat our phrase like a broken record until Mrs. Cristina, desperate, would come out of her house and shout at us, like a madwoman.

The other day, however, someone stole her ring — the one with the solitaire — and my troubles began...

So, when the teacher Giacomina told me that I had to color all the parrots at the bottom of my album because they would look more beautiful that way, I did it, also tracing Mrs. Cristina with this message:

"I can't take your ring out because I don't have it!"

Two Particular Carabinieri

– CHAPTER 4 –

A few days after the theft, two special carabinieri arrived at the school. I prefer number two because it is even; odd numbers, on the other hand, create problems for me since there is always one left alone, and I don't know what to do with it.

My father says that the carabinieri are indeed good people, but he prefers the police officers to them. To be precise, he prefers the policewomen. Recently, he has developed a great liking for Commissioner Lolita Lobosco, known as Lolì, from the Bari Homicide squad, whom he admires on TV. He says that she solves desperate cases and that she is also a *true female*. I like beautiful women too, and I got a little worried. Not for anything else, but because of my mother, who every now and then bursts out:

"Yeeeeees... men, as soon as they see a woman, they all become *blundering fools!*"

I was there thinking about this word for a long time, which my mother uses when men run after women. In the end, I concluded that my father and I are also two of those fools. But the fact remains that, instead of Commissioner Lolita, two very special carabinieri came to look for me at school. And this is called bad luck.

The other day, when I entered the computer lab, where I usually work with the professor, I found them in front of me. They looked at me several times, intrigued by my dangling, unusual walk. Then, as if struck by my presence, they came closer. They were very nice and asked me a lot of questions like, *"Hey, boy, what's your name?"* and *"Do you attend this school?"* and again, *"How old are you?"* But I didn't answer because I don't talk to strangers.

Dominique, my support teacher who is obsessed with flowers, told me that it is normal to be questioned in the event of a theft. Therefore, I had to answer without fear.

From TV shows, I learned that the carabinieri typically intervene in cases of robbery, murder, or any other offenses that don't come to mind right now; in short, when someone breaks the law. I hadn't done any of this, so I could rest assured.

Perhaps the carabinieri had already spoken to my classmates too. However, I didn't ask because my mother always advises me to mind my own business.

So, I paused to observe the laces of their shoes, when one of them addressed me:

"So, young man, will you tell us your name?"

At first, I felt lost because of those chicks that I felt running in my head and that created anxiety. Then, being careful in spelling first the name and then the surname, I pronounced, "T-o-b-i-a - B-a-r-b-a-t-o".

"Hell, I was beginning to think you didn't have the tongue to answer..." barked the one with the shortest lace, trying to be kind. Then he added:

"What day were you born?"

"I-was-born-on-Mon-day," I replied, shifting my gaze from their shoelaces to a black stain on the floor.

Spraying tiny bubbles of saliva on my face, the carabiniere did not give up:

"Yes, okay, but how old are you?"

I remained silent for a minute and five seconds and, still looking at the floor, I said:

"I-am-seven-teen-years-old."

Then, the other carabiniere added:

"Hey, Tobia, we're not going to hurt you; we just want to know why you're bothering Mrs. Martinez?"

Those two were asking me too many questions all at once, which made my head start to falter. Still, I answered anyway.

"I don't-know-Mrs.-Marti-nez."

As I answered, I kept my gaze on the black stains on the floor; they were the chewing gums that my friend Pilù always spat onto the ground. Just the other day he got a stern reprimand from the school janitor because, when he cleans, the broom gets punctually stuck to them. And this pisses him off.

"Mrs. Martinez says otherwise," said the carabiniere, perched on the chair. Then he continued, "Aren't you Tobia Barbato?"

That was a good question since he had just called me by that name! My father was right: the carabinieri could not really be trusted, especially when there were two of them.

"So, are you really sure you don't know Mrs. Cristina Martinez and her parrot?" insisted one of the two again, trying to get into my good graces.

At the word parrot, I raised my head. Now he had spoken clearly! It was Mrs. Cristina who had sent the carabinieri to school. But I still didn't understand. What did I have to do with Mrs. Cristina?

"Hmm-yes-I-know-her," I replied, drooling a little.

"Damn, boy, then it was you who stole her ring!" pressed the shorter and fatter carabiniere, like a perfect snooper, making his lower lip tremble. His lower lip always trembled when he pronounced the word *ring*.

It was only then that I learned the truth: Mrs. Cristina had denounced me, keeping her promise, convinced that I had stolen her ring with the solitaire.

"Come on, young man, answer!" reiterated the other, calmly holding his overflowing belly.

"So, what?" they both said, at last, resting their hands on my shoulders.

When I felt their hands brush against my body, I took a step back. I don't like physical contact, and to be safe, I put a nice gap between me and them. And before Dominique could stop me, I hit my forehead with two punches; that was definitely a difficult day.

My mom says that the carabinieri are stand-up people, so there was no need to lose patience. However, if that happened, I should have put my hands in my pockets instead of hitting myself and screaming.

All nonsense because, under these circumstances, I completely forget my good intentions. So, I shouted an answer:

"I-didn't-take-the-ring-of-Mrs-Cristi-na; I hate-rings." Then, I took off my shoes, covered my eyes with the palm of my hand, and began to swing like a pendulum, resting now on my right leg, now on my left leg.

"So, if you didn't steal that ring, who took it?" asked the fat one, perplexed.

"Yes, then who stole it?" echoed the other, scratching his head and wrinkling his nose. So saying, they closed the report in a black folder with a red border and, as my father says, they went away like two old chanterelle mushrooms.

I continued swinging until I heard a car drive away.

It was a Fiat Bravo with an engine of 1900 cubic capacity; I would have bet on it!

When you are Sad, Sing!

At home, I found my mother, who attempted to hold me in her arms to convey her love and her disbelief in the story of the theft.

But I screamed first, then ran away.

The hug, although it is an affectionate gesture, makes me feel as though I am in a death trap; this makes me feel sad and nervous. Therefore, between one caress and another, my mom always ventures:

"Sooner or later, Tobia, you'll have to get used to my hugs!" Or: "Come, let's try again. I promise not to hurt you. You'll see that if you resist, your willpower will be rewarded in the end."

Then, turning to my father, she usually adds:

"I believe it will rain. Today, Tobia is anxious. He is very sensitive to weather changes!"

And my father always replies dryly:

"Don't talk nonsense. Can you explain what hugs have to do with climate change?"

Nevertheless, neither of them wants to understand that my behavior, which the psychologist categorizes as part of behavioral stereotypies, provides me with security. In short, refusing hugs or caresses, as I have already explained, prevents me from feeling bad and to some extent protects me from discomfort. However, they do not seem to understand this.

Even my father, in terms of stereotypies, is not joking. And he is also stubborn!

When he undresses, he folds his clothes carefully and always in the same order: first the sweater, then the shirt, and then the trousers. When he gets dressed, he puts on trousers first, followed by the shirt, and then the sweater. No one dares to contradict him. My brothers, on the other hand, leave their clothes scattered all over the house, and when they can't find them, they scream.

Tell me if this is not stereotypy too!

Fortunately, Mom jokes about it. She always says that ours is not a normal family because we are all nuttier than fruitcakes. Whenever something bad happens, she reacts philosophically, bursting out laughing, to say the least, heroically. So, when the school principal called to inform us that two carabinieri had questioned me because they suspected I had stolen Mrs. Cristina Martinez's ring, and that he had summoned her and my father to school, my mother, with her proverbial calm, replied in rhyme:

"My God! How dare they call my child a thief? He may be careless, but he is never a thief! Don't you think, Mr. Principal, that my son has already been punished enough with this accusation of theft?"

However, the Principal defended himself by stating that specific rules had to be followed. He had nothing to do with it; the carabinieri had formulated the accusation.

Nevertheless, when she set the phone handset down, my mother sighed and looked at me as if she were seeing me for the first time. She remained silent for ten minutes, with her hands in her hair; then, shaking off her certainties, she tried to find out the truth from me.

I fiddled with the laces of my jumpsuit for a long time, then chewed them by softening them with saliva. Her questions had made me uncomfortable, so much so that I began to rock slowly at first, then harder and harder. Ultimately, seeing me agitated and sensing that something was going on in my head, she said to me:

"Okay, Tobia, it's all okay. Let's forget it... for me, you are and remain innocent. What do you say, though, if we try to put your head in order? I'm sure you can do it, perhaps by writing or singing about your discomforts!

My mom always knows what to do in difficult situations. She consistently manages to shatter that crystal ball in which I confine myself like a prisoner. But that day, I didn't want to start singing, as I usually did when I felt cheerful. So, just to do something, I began to doodle in my notebook. I tried to write a poem that included the words parrot and carabinieri, but I couldn't find any rhyme.

In the end, I felt tired and stressed with so many chicks with matted hair in my brain, so much so that I hated the parrot, the carabinieri, the School Principal, and Mrs. Cristina because they were the cause of my troubles. Fed up, I crouched under the kitchen table, my favorite place, and stayed there for hours, rocking myself.

Crawling like a snake, I picked up my notebook, sat down on the kitchen chair, and thought of the teacher Giacomina, who had taught me to compose poems. I thought I heard her voice:

"Several words that are on the same line form the verse, from the Latin term *vertere*, which means to turn. More verses form the stanza...," but the one I had finally managed to scribble on the paper, personified a cloud and was a calligram, but still a poem.

clouds

right over

under a veil cover

and the Saturnine   *haze*

hides them   *nowadays*

When I read it to my mother, she explained that over and cover, haze, and *nowadays* form the couplet rhymes: different words that end with the same sound.

I began to feel calmer. While waiting for Giacomina to arrive, my mother said:

"Come on, Tobia, let's try to find meaning in some words..."

Then she paused for a moment to find them in her head. Seeing her struggle, I shouted:

"Yes, I know... Mom, it's old age that makes you forget things! Who... I don't know!?"

"Oh, Tobia, what are you saying? Do you really think I'm old?" she replied, amused. Before she began writing again, she pulled me closer to her for yet another moment of affection, just as she had before. I struggle to tolerate these displays of affection, so I turned away from her and said:

"I was just joking, Mom; I was just messing with you!"

She burst out laughing, and while doing so with gusto, she did not give up:

"Come on, come on, describe the meaning of these words!" she said, slipping the paper under my nose and forcing me to read: The double, The oasis, The man purse, The cafeteria.

It appeared to be a difficult task, but then I wrote:

The double = are two Tobias put together.

The oasis = is the place where my mother wants to escape when she says: "I would like to escape to an oasis."

The man purse = is the bag where I collect all my toys.

The cafeteria = is where you eat, which reminds me of the cakes I eat with Giacomina.

Then we moved on to consonants, where I learned that the f flies, the l is soft, the m is smooth, the s rustles, the r runs, the t is big-headed, the gr is angry, the gn is padded, and the sh is slippery!

Finally, Mom moved on to the words she called "alive" and, with her help, divided them by category:

In the fatty words I placed: *thigh, pork, and butter.*

In the pointed words: nail, needle, and awl.

In the soft words: *cloud, cushion, ring.*

In the harsh words, however, I inserted: **Cristina, parrot, and carabinieri.**

The most beautiful words I ultimately wrote are these:

I love you, Mom.

My Mom, Just like the Phoenix

— CHAPTER 6 —

Life is not easy for those with older siblings, even if it means always having a partner to play with or someone to rely on. However, I love to be alone, and this is one of the issues that separates me from my family.

Those without siblings cannot understand the quarrels that break out over a toy or, more simply, over who should occupy a particular seat on the sofa. I have two brothers: Hector and Matthew. Hector is my older brother. He is very tall and thin and already chases after the girls. His masculine face is framed by a cascade of blond hair swept back, which bounces with every step, and on his chest he sports a tuft of hair that resembles a frightened cat. He loves to wear black clothing, such as shirts, T-shirts, and pants. This means that, since I do not like the color black, I secretly cut up all his clothes with scissors. This is how the wars of pushing and punching break out in my house, forcing my parents to endure real battles to separate us. But he is too strong, and we end up rolling on the floor, where he hugs me so tightly that I freeze and come out defeated.

Then there is Matthew. He is only a few years older than I am, loves me very much, but like all brothers, he always wants to win. Even though he defines himself as a grown-up, he still collects vintage cars that he locks in his closet, making it difficult for me to set some of them free. But one day, after so much noise, I managed to get hold of a beautiful red Ferrari, which I have now lost. He called me a thief, so I jumped on him and hit him; I couldn't stand that insult. First, I spat, and then, with the precision of a boxer, I delivered a right hand that he skillfully parried. My father, who can't stand so much revelry, began to preach the usual sermon after this particularly violent quarrel, staring at us sternly with tight lips as if a burp had soured his mouth.

Even this morning, I had a fight with Matthew. I got up feeling quite angry and, following my instincts, I unmade the bed I had just made, flushed the toilets, unrolled the toilet paper, turned on the taps to hear the water downpour, scattered all my household items, and finally took off my shoes. I always take off my shoes when I'm anxious.

It's my way of protesting, even if my mother says that sometimes I behave like a fool. This happens when I'm tense and can't make myself understood.

When I heard the word "thief," the issue of the ring resurfaced in my mind.

Being labeled a thief is not something I appreciate, and now that the news has spread, people have voiced their opinions. I have heard individuals express:

"Yes, oh well, he didn't do it on purpose. The boy should be understood; they don't see that it is so...!"

Or:

"Eh, but you have to educate him. At least, make him understand that you are not supposed to steal!"

So, the first punch was caught by my brother Matthew, who, in reality, made the only mistake of picking up my scattered toys and turning off the water taps. An endless quarrel ensued, and if Mom hadn't separated us, I would have scratched his face. As usual, he threatened to leave home if my parents did not take serious measures against me. My father then intervened and, going straight to the point, urged:

"Hey, you two, calm down and no more bullshit!"

"Oh, my little one, what's wrong?" my mother complained, turning to me.

Then again, I can't stand her when she calls me *little*.

"Well, I knew it would end like this!" my father sentenced, while Hector disappeared, and Matthew argued poorly.

In the end, my mother got annoyed and said that she just could not take it anymore regarding our behavior, and that all of us in the family must improve our manners.

But in my mind (at that moment), many thoughts gathered all at once: I recalled Mrs. Cristina's parrot, the stolen ring, the carabinieri's suspicion that I was a thief, and the quarrel with my brother. At that point, a cold sweat began to run down my spine and, following my instincts, I took the kitchen chair and hurled it through the air, with my father telling me:

"Hey, hey, my friend, what the hell are you doing? Wait, wait, we're all going to get hurt here!"

Then, I began moaning, hitting my head, rolling my eyes, slump-ing to the ground, and gnashing my teeth.

I was in that state for several minutes, until Mom tried to calm me down, whispering to me:

"Come on, come on, Tobia, pull yourself together! Make peace with your brother. Even if the theft matter is serious, your father will discuss it with the warrant officer of the carabinieri. He will explain to him that it was not you who stole the ring and that, therefore, they should look for the thief elsewhere. We will show that, although you are a kleptomaniac, you are not a thief. I know you are telling the truth!"

"We needed this other problem," my father replied, slamming the door and walking away.

Even though my mother had uttered that strange word (*klepto-maniac*), the meaning of which I have not yet understood, I thought that finally someone was beginning to reason at home. As usual, this someone is always her. My mom, after a while, managed to imprison me in her arms and curb my agitation. Then, to give me security, she whispered to me a thousand times that she loved me.

I felt a little guilty for what I had done. And when my mother asked me if I loved her too, mortified, I looked at the wound I had caused on her wrist, biting her during that moment of anger, and, to overcome the annoyance that her hug was causing me, I gritted my teeth and remained motionless.

As Giacomina says, my mother is like the Arabian phoenix: she has the strength to rise over and over from her ashes. She always complains that she has reached her patience limit, but at the right moment, she shows such strength and determination that amazes everyone. She manages family affairs effortlessly and, at just the right time, with a snip, she puts everyone in line, including me.

At that point, peace had already been attained, but the problem remained: who had stolen Mrs. Cristina's ring?

I stayed up most of the night trying to solve the mystery, but in the end, I had to turn off the light and bury my head under the pillow to avoid hearing my father's snoring, which, by God, is so loud it sounds like an electric saw constantly at work.

Holidays in Porretta Terme

Giacomina, my teacher who follows me home like a shadow, always says that I am a smart boy. To help me understand that whatever she says is not baloney, and to give me confidence, she made me write it in blood red in my notebook.

I stained all the papers; however, in the end, I succeeded.

I wrote: TOBIA IS A SMART GUY. But she punctually corrected: **I AM A SMART GUY.**

I also wrote that my father is an idiot because he broke his car. The fact is that I hate knowing our car is broken because it makes me anxious, and I end up getting wet. Ultimately, we argue because my father, in turn, cannot stand my anxiety.

"You have to have respect for your parents, even if they are not always right," said Giacomina, scolding me.

Then, she explained to me that arguing with one's parents is normal because it reflects the classic conflict between father and son: a typical problem of adolescence. I don't really understand what conflict means, but I think it's a kind of war in which there is never a winner.

If that's the case, I'd like to be a mechanic in life; at least I can repair my father's car and prevent him from feeling frustrated when it breaks down.

The term " frustrated " is not a choice of mine, but his. He uses it every time his car leaves him stranded, which happens often. Once, the carburetor threw a tantrum, deserting him in the garage. To get out, he was forced to call the tow truck. Another time, the clutch broke, and I am not here to describe what happened. My father got furious because he had to spend a lot of money. He always swears that he will sell that car, sooner or later, but he only says it and never does it.

Therefore, I console myself by breaking down and repairing my cars to understand how they are constructed inside. Then again, I lose some parts, and my mother is forced to repair the models with tape. As far as I understand, my father's Fiat Croma this time broke the crankshaft. This means that the mechanic should fix it; however, my father says he has a butt face because he asks for a lot of money. Then again, the car always breaks down. He also concludes that any mechanics who don't know their job well have a butt face.

I laughed so hard at this idea that I wet myself. Of course, the term used by my father was just a figure of speech.

This incident of getting wet has happened before; not my fault, of course, but I couldn't keep my anxiety in check.

Another time, for example, it happened when we went on vacation. We traveled over seven hundred kilometers because Porretta Terme is quite far from my home. It took us many hours to arrive, and just before reaching the hotel, the car began to sob. Since we risked being stranded, we stopped at the first mechanic, who underestimated the severity of the breakdown. Therefore, we ended up stuck on the road anyway.

My father began to grumble, and as he was having a nervous breakdown, he inhaled deeply.

"Holy shit! Is it possible that these mechanics all have a butt face?!" he said at the end, sounding quite resigned.

Then, I began to laugh and feel impatient. Usually, I'm not very inclined to long trips because they tire me out. When I get tired, I repeatedly ask, "When are we going home?" or "Why are we here?" Even worse, I never mention that I need to pee because I was taught not to use other people's bathrooms. So, it turned out that even at that time, I wet myself.

"Fuck, Tobia, do you want to break the record for the longest pee?" my father screamed, seeing me all wet and at the limit of endurance. In the meantime, my mother tried to block the lake I had created with a towel hurriedly pulled from my personal backpack.

Apart from these accidents, I felt good in Porretta. As my father proudly announced, we stayed in a large five-star hotel where everything was perfect, featuring a sparkling restaurant and waiters in white livery who revered me as a young lord. My mother, who usually doesn't care much about her appearance, got dolled up that evening. She also styled her hair, which cascaded from her head like the tentacles of a curled octopus; she even adorned her finger with a large solitaire ring.

I was stunned because it reminded me of Mrs. Cristina's ring. But she readily said:

"Oh, Tobia, I know what you're thinking, but it's not what it is; solitaires are all similar."

Then, she added:

"Tobia, please don't go near the other tables to beg for something. Sit and eat in a proper manner. Don't suck on spaghetti like a chicken's ass, as is your custom, because you sprinkle sauce all over the place!"

She said that while putting on a lot of airs. Then she called the waiter.

"For Tobia, a nice plate of spaghetti, please!" she ordered, in a caressing voice, while two flies danced on her face.

When I eat spaghetti, I like to twist it with a fork, so much so that I have become exceptionally good at it. That evening, I surpassed myself: I ate greedily, staining abundantly the new shirt I had just worn. I only needed one, just one forkful, and my mouth was filled like a suitcase. I tried to swallow the bite, but I could not. Before I suffocated to death, I vomited everything on the table.

In that great uproar, my brothers attempted to pretend nothing had happened, while my father, who followed me with repressed anger, did his best to deliver two blows like boulders to my shoulder.

Then, through clenched teeth, he said to my mother:

"Take him away, or I'll kill him!"

To justify that incident, my mother began distributing smiles to the diners who looked at us with pitiful eyes. Finally, overwhelmed by the tension, she pulled me like a spring toward the bathroom. Meanwhile, I found it very funny and began to laugh out loud, so much so that, once again, I wet myself.

Well, the next day my father worked hard to get us home, making excuses that the car kept throwing tantrums and that this old fox of a mechanic had already caused enough trouble.

I Hate
Detective Stories

– CHAPTER 8 –

"It takes faith in life to overcome the darkest difficulties," Dominique said softly, sounding much like a cat that had just finished eating a mouse, so as not to disturb the literature teacher who was trying to make a rather serious speech in a very noisy class.

"I would like to see you in my place, when a *pain in the ass* accuses you of theft!" I stammered, drooling a little. And when I drool, the result of my speech is always disastrous.

I had heard the phrase "pain in the ass" from Pilù, and since I liked it, I repeated it several times while referring to the carabinieri.

Dominique smiled. Then he repeated:

"Pain in the ass, huh!? Who teaches you these words?"

I didn't respond because I was annoyed that the news that I was a kleptomaniac who had stolen Mrs. Cristina's ring and pulled her parrot's neck had spread throughout the school. So, everyone looked at me with a blend of curiosity and suspicion, and I couldn't stand nosy people.

A few days later, the two carabinieri returned to school for a classic search, asking questions of all the boys who usually stopped near Mrs. Cristina's house to tease the parrot. Since they were there, they also rummaged through my support room.

When I saw them enter, I began to walk in zigzags and then started to rock; I also spat in the air, but I kept the words "pain in the ass" to myself, as Dominique had recommended. If my friend Pilù hadn't given me his hand to reassure me, maybe I would have even run away...

Suddenly, I turned around and said to Dominique:

"I'm tired. These-two-don't-understand-the-problem,-don't-find-solutions. They don't-listen to me. I'm really fed up!"

Laughing, he raised his right hand, crossing his fingers as a sign of good luck. Then, he answered:

Tobia, what are you worried about? It's just a formality. And you're here for clarification; you haven't run away! Everything will be fine; listen to me.

I know well that I can't run away when there is an on-going investigation; otherwise, I will be presumed guilty, and I am not guilty.

The professor allowed the two carabinieri to enter a classroom where I usually stop to do my manual work with him. There are always several chairs, a wardrobe, and a table topped with a ceramic vase filled with fresh flowers, which I throw out of the window as soon as I can because they remind me of Mrs. Cristina. Then, Dominique called the suspects one at a time, including my classmate, Maria. I was called last.

"What's your name?" the younger carabiniere asked me again.

I looked at the thick, black hair on his nose, protruding like bushes. I knew he was already aware of my name and age, so I chose not to respond.

The two then contemplated it and, looking at me directly in the face, exclaimed together:

"Ah, you're the guy we interrogated the other day. The young Tobia Barbato, aren't you?"

"Yes," I replied.

"What do you have in that man purse? It seems so full..." they asked me with curiosity.

"It's-my-man purse. I-have-inside-my-things. I-always carry them-with-me."

"Can you show us what's inside?" they both said, holding out their hands.

I curled up in my chair and bobbed my head to nod firmly. But they insisted, so much so that I reluctantly slipped it off my shoulder.

That man purse, made of black faux leather, was purchased by my mother from a Chinese stall last summer. She was desperate, watching me fill my trouser pockets with items every time we went out. Besides that, I dislike others snooping into my stuff.

The taller of the two carabinieri, the one who was always sweaty and blocked my passage with his belly, opened the zipper and, disregarding my anxiety, emptied the contents onto the table. Then, with his chunky, hairy hands, he verbalized:

- ten pens, pencils, and paints
- two pocket calendars
- different shoelaces
- a bunch of keys
- a toy car wheel
- a non-working mobile phone
- a red and a green screwdriver
- a red and a blue ball
- a kitchen toothbrush
- two oranges, a bit rotten
- many unidentifiable objects, and...
- A solid gold ring with a gemstone!

My mother would have called it a real collection of junk.

I gazed at the ring with curiosity. It was indeed golden, and the stone set in it, as large as the nail on my middle finger, emanated a certain glow.

"Hmm... And this... Hmm... What is it?" said the two men together. They spoke slowly, so much so that they sounded like two stutterers.

"One-ring," I replied, rather confused. Then I seemed to recognize it. "It's-lady-Cristina's-ring!" I added, chanting.

"Aaah, well, good. Do you know what that means?" said the one with the bushy nose hair, pacing up and down the room. "That you are the only suspect!"

"Well, well. So, we can consider the case solved!" added the other, displaying a row of yellow teeth.

Mrs. Cristina's ring had been recovered, and the story would finally end. I felt genuinely happy. However, at that moment, the case began to get complicated because I had become the only suspect.

If *the body of the crime*, as they called the ring, had been found in my man purse, by law, it was obvious that I was also the thief.

I saw the faces of the two make a grimace of happiness, just like my father does when he discovers that he has earned several euros on the Scratch card. At that point, I tried to understand:

First: The ring had been found.
Second: The thief was not me.
Third: This story was turning into a detective story.
Fourth: I hate Detective Stories.

But My Mother Likes Detective Stories

I'm not a great reader, you got that. When I have a book in my hands, I tend to make it into small pieces or strips, especially if I have an awl or a pen with me. I enjoy pricking the pages, which I then tear and wet with saliva or soap bubbles. This is a ritual that brings me immense pleasure! Those who don't understand this are ready to reproach me because it's something you are not supposed to do.

The family writer, on the other hand, is my mother, who, when she is not taking care of the house and escaping the assaults of us children, devours books. In the sense that she reads everything. Her favorites are detective stories. These days, I see her focused, as you say, on two thrillers: "The Murders of the Rue Morgue" by Edgar Allan Poe, the absolute inventor of the detective story, and "The Murder of the Rue Saint-Roch" by the French writer Alexandre Dumas.

Stated this way, it may seem unimportant; however, listening to my mother, I realized that the two stories, published a few years apart and written by different authors, are fundamentally the same in content! So much so that, in the end, she commented:

My God, Tobia, you should read them; they are a mystery within a mystery! It would be exciting to find out which of the two copied the other. In reflection, an intrigue of no small importance has been created. Now I ask myself, who holds the record for the inventor of the Detective Story, Poe – as I have always known – or Dumas? A tough nut to crack!

While she remained immersed in this boring puzzle, continuing to talk to herself as crazy people do, trying to figure out which of the two had copied the other's work in such a brazen way, I kept blowing on the plastic stick loaded with soap, releasing dozens of bubbles into the air. They danced up and down, like butterflies, and I hopped there to make them burst before they hit the ground. However, my mother's boring tirade continued to get on my nerves for her detailed explanations of thrillers, *noir,* and more typical subgenres such as *detective stories for young people...*

Just the other day, as if that were not enough, she asked me:

"Tobia, do you want to read a little with me? Teacher Giacomina would be very happy to see you so busy."

"Ugh, what are you reading this time?" I grumbled suspiciously.

"Cherries at Midnight — The Diary of a Thirteen-Year-Old Girl." The author is Giulia Poli Disanto, an Italian. Don't worry, it has nothing to do with the previous two. You know, it's a funny, lively book. It is the diary of a typical teenager with her turmoil..."

Then, noticing that I was gazing at her with expressionless eyes, she halted abruptly. I always look this way when I don't understand complicated speeches.

"You're right..." she continued, pulling me toward her.

At that contact, even if it was my mother's, I stiffened slightly. Ignoring my behavior, she continued:

"Come on, Tobia, sit down here beside me," and, nailing me to a chair, she added:

"The protagonist is Priscilla. Many characters revolve around her: a little "troublemaker" sister, Cree Cree; her mother; her grandmother, Priscilla; her father; an older brother, wise and nerdy at the right moments; and the Romanian caregiver. All these elements compose a family picture that diminishes and overcomes difficulties, making them almost pleasant and providing us with flashes of great fun and joy."

At that point, I sneezed so hard that I sprayed saliva on the pages of the book. If I had had a pen or a pencil at hand, I would have pierced them with real pleasure. But Mom, instinctively, wiped my saliva with the flap of her sweater's sleeve. Afterward, she complained:

"Tobia, you never have a handkerchief in your pocket! You have smeared all the pages on me!" Without giving me a chance to move, she attacked again:

"What was I saying? Ah, yes, that it's very funny and that Priscilla's dad is resigned and slightly awkward. The little sister, on the other hand, is vibrant and intuitive; the older brother is a bit opinionated; and the mother, who always has a solution ready for everything and everyone, is wise and aware! Ah! The trip to Paris was hilarious, and the forgetfulness of the grandmother suffering from Alzheimer's, along with the investigations into the end of the parrot Picasso! The most surprising thing is that this diary becomes a Detective Story... Yes, yes. It's a mystery, you know... Tobia, can you hear me...?"

"Can I get up now?" I replied, trying to keep at bay the first chicks I felt invading my head: I wanted to escape her explanations...

When my mother starts telling a story, she never finishes it. At that moment, I really wanted to get up and pee, but she insisted, keeping me imprisoned in the chair.

"The "revelation" in the final part makes it intriguing and surprises the reader who neither expects nor suspects this twist!"

"**Another parrot? Another Mystery?**" I yelled, hopping into my chair. "Ugh, I hate parrots, and I hate detective stories too, you know!" I replied, peeing all over myself.

"Too bad!" she replied. Then she added: "Tobia, I guarantee you that it is a different detective story than usual; it's really funny! You should try to read it... It's not really one of those stories you don't like... Here, I found the exact definition. We'll call it "Funthriller" instead of "Detective story for young adults, OK?". The two protagonists, Cree-Cree and her sister Priscilla, manage to discover the killer while they are binging on cherries and..."

My mother continued to talk about this or that detective story, even ventilating that difficult term, as she likes to say in English, because it is chic. However, she did not finish explaining because she looked at my trousers, which had a large dark halo in front of them. When she finally let me go — I, who had now let myself go completely — left a conspicuous puddle under the chair.

Yellow, too...

Teacher
Giacomina

– CHAPTER 10 –

The teacher Giacomina is a failed pastry chef. When I feel collaborative, we prepare many fruit desserts, which we then eat together. I enjoy making cakes because I have a lot of fun with flour; I like to sprinkle it all over the house. However, she then forces me to clean, and again she tells me:

"Tobia, now take the red recipe book and write down the doses!"

Yesterday, we prepared orange fritters, even though the original recipe called for apples. I chose oranges because I like them, and every time I cut them in half, it feels as if the Sun magically appears to me. However, a big mess occurred: while frying them, the juice caused boiling oil to splatter everywhere. Then I thought that oranges are the tears of the sun. When I told Giacomina, we laughed so much...

This is the recipe I created:

Ingredients for two people:

Two oranges, one egg, one ounce of 00 flour, a pinch of salt, some maraschino liqueur, sugar to taste, powdered sugar to cover, and half a large glass of vegetable oil.

With Giacomina, I peeled and sliced the oranges, allowing them to macerate in maraschino already sprinkled with sugar. Then I prepared the batter with an egg, a tablespoon of oil, flour, a pinch of salt, and a splash of maraschino.

Giacomina heated the remaining oil in a pan, and, with her help, I dipped the orange slices first in the batter and placed them in the pan. We obtained golden disks that we sprinkled with powdered sugar. Then we ate them. They were delicious!

We have set aside so many of those recipes that we could open a pastry shop. My mother is pleased about this because she sees that I am happy.

However, when I am nervous and unable to express myself, the teacher Giacomina has me fill out a form in which I simply mark the adjective that best describes my mood. For example:

TOBIA IS
* Happy * Tired * Serene * Worried * Sensitive * Available
* Violent * Willing * Angry * Proud * Beautiful * Solar
 * Sad * Rested * Shy * Nervous * Anxious * Listless
 * Sociable * Ugly * Kind   or * ???????? (?)

But that day I didn't want to choose. I took up my pen and, with uncertain scribble, which Giacomina defined as crow's feet, I wrote: TOBIA IS NOT A THIEF!!

She immediately corrected: I AM NOT A THIEF!!

"We all know you're not a thief," she replied, hugging me. Then, smiling, she added: "Wait, I have something for you. It's a book. A special book, which we will read together... You know, the protagonist is a guy who, in some ways, looks like you. He is very smart. Just think that he manages to solve a particularly complicated case, such as the murder of a dog." And as she said that, she pulled a Mark Haddon novel with a very long title out of her bag: "The Curious Incident of the Dog in the Night-Time."

It seemed like a conspiracy. So, at the sight, I reacted:

"No-Giacomina-no. You're stressing me out with all these detective stories!"

But she, fussy as always, did not give in:

"Reading, my little one, helps you grow. Remember! I'm sure, however, that you will have a lot of fun when we read it. Christopher, the protagonist's name, is a smart boy, just like you, who improvises as an investigator and manages to solve the case."

In the end, tired of listening to that stubborn teacher, I gave up, and together we read the book. It proved to be a helpful read because I understood that I am not the only one who has certain fixations...

After I had successfully read that book, my mother one day recognized that Giacomina had been the only person who had managed to find the right key to open my heart.

But you know, people are not all the same. Each of us has characteristics that make us sympathetic or unpleasant, and I liked Giacomina very much.

One day, playing with my mother, she said to me:

"Your teacher Giacomina is a really good person, Tobia."

"She is five-star, like the hotel in Porretta Terme!" I replied, remembering the comparison my father had made about the quality of hotels.

"Yes, of course, but she is not a hotel. She is a person as loving and warm as she is intuitive and tender, even if she has the defect of splitting hairs four ways, with her fussiness!"

In this, I agreed with my mother. She had been the only person I had allowed to touch, caress, and hug me. Later, if I permitted my parents to do so, I owed it solely to her and to that fussiness of hers...

Giacomina always knew how to treat me. She understood everything about me. She knew when I was happy and when, instead, those strange chicks were about to arrive in my head, which made me anxious and angry. She never addressed me with all those nonsensical expressions that others said referring to me, such as, for example, "elusive eel" or "shy snail." I owe it to her if I have learned that kisses, caresses, and hugs are nothing more than manifestations of affection.

That day, when she presented me with that card, I was quite agitated, and my teacher noticed. To gain insight into my true state of mind, she added eight question marks to the table. I contemplated this for a moment, then added a ninth question mark in parentheses. After that, I wrote a simple expression with an odd number of letters: TOBIA is p i s s e d o f f.

Then I banged my fist on the table, and the colored pencils, which had all been lined up to color the umpteenth bird that this time was a jackdaw and therefore black, rolled one by one onto the ground. I opened my hand and, without thinking twice, threw the bird to the floor as well.

Giacomina then corrected, "TOBIA is worried."

I copied it exactly: TOBIA is worried.

Giacomina then continued in this game: Why is Tobia worried?

I replied, "Because he is considered a ring thief and risks going to prison!"

My teacher wrote again: "The days are divided into good and bad. I see that this is a bad day for Tobia. I don't believe that Tobia is a thief. Tobia is an intelligent and kind guy, but above all, he is an honest guy: he is my champion!"

I read those words and smiled. Then, I put an end to that fun with a phrase I rarely write and usually dedicate to my mother; so I wrote again: *"Tobia loves you!"*

Giacomina corrected: *"I love you!"*

But I felt the need to tell her in my own words and, doing my best, I said:

"Do you know, Giacomina, that I love you?"

"Tobia, what are you doing? Are you kidding me?" she replied, gathering my hands in hers.

"No. No. No. I love you because you took my wet hands and I dried them in yours, and now I'm better!"

At that point, she stroked my hair, and I let her do it. "Oh, little one!" she exclaimed, and her hands were warm and light. They were like two butterfly wings. They reminded me of my mother's hands when she tries to caress me and calls me little.

Suddenly, I felt happy and, without anyone forcing me, I picked up the colored pencils that had scattered on the ground. I made sure to eliminate the black pencil because I don't like it; it's as dark as darkness, and I'm afraid of the dark.

I arranged them in a semicircle, one next to the other. When I finally finished picking them up, there was a beautiful rainbow on the table.

My School

Today I feel like an animal in a cage. No one understands me.

They don't let me play with saliva or soap bubbles because I spill water everywhere, and not even with my wet paper strips. They don't let me entertain myself, nothing at all. They just say that it has to be done.

I believe it's entirely due to the accident of the other day. My father is still upset about the broken chair. Also, I despise not being able to enjoy my paper strips during the day.

Usually, I don't take orders from anyone. I'm a free guy, you know. But everyone says that I must obey the rules because I'm growing up, and growing up means I have to be strong and not revert to the usual stereotypies, such as soaking the paper with saliva or hurling chairs in the air when I get nervous.

Apart from these inconveniences, I am improving because I can now do several things at the same time: for example, having a snack and getting ready to go out, if I don't have any other big trouble.

Once, when I was much younger, I carried out the actions of the day as I pleased, and what was normal for me was not normal for daily life. For example, I liked to go to sleep very late at night, with my mother threatening:

"It's already eleven o'clock; fuck, Tobia, go to bed!"

Or in the morning, when everyone got up and I stayed asleep, and she pleaded:

"It's ten o'clock, are you getting up or what?"

My mind was very confused, and Giacomina, to bring order to my daily gestures, urged me to create a roadmap. She told me it was called that, although I couldn't immediately understand why it was called so, since there was no map or road on the paper...

Then Giacomina explained to me that the roadmap is a simple, ordered list of actions to be completed during the day.

I thought of the letters of the alphabet and associated them with an action of the day:

A: get up in the morning and unmake the bed.

B: pee or poop.

C: at eight o'clock take the vitamins with a glass of water (even if I drain the bottle).

D: wash my face, hands, body (with my father yelling: "Take a shower first!")

E: have breakfast with cinnamon soy milk and cookies (the cookies must always be the same and in number of four).

F: brush my teeth.

G: dress myself.

H: go to school.

I: come back from school.

L: have lunch.

M: listen to music.

N: rest.

O: do my homework.

P: have dinner.

Q: go to bed.

R: Amen, end of the day and of my alphabet!

I have other teachers at school. I consider them two-star tea-chers because they struggle to keep up with me, even though they are friendly and nice. I curl up on the desk and cover my mouth with my hands because the noise and confusion disorient me. Sometimes, I rock or make a siren-like sound. Other times, however, I plug my ears, close my eyes, and tuck my head into my shoulders, just like my turtles Brilly and Loly do when I insist on feeding them lettuce. My psychologist says that my brain goes haywire when it is faced with numerous questions or when asked to perform several actions simultaneously.

My school corresponds to the letter H and is even-numbered in the order of the alphabet. This means that I go there willingly. It also corresponds to the symbol — H — that Dominique has behind the door of our workshop, which means Handicap. However, the story of the ring theft spread throughout the school and compromised my good intentions and enthusiasm to go willingly; this led me to make another big mess...

The other day, some classmates asked me if it was true that Mrs. Cristina's ring had been found in my man purse. Giovanni yanked me in an attempt to grab it, and I didn't like this at all.

"Even if the ring was stolen by him, we'll never know," he said, assuming my guilt.

I was already on alert when I felt a tremor in my leg, something very similar to an electric current. I couldn't control it as I kicked the door with my foot, creating a large hole. Then, with a vigorous fist, I hit my friend in the chest so hard that we rolled on the ground, clinging to each other.

I wanted to stop, but I couldn't. So, I panicked, which made me even more nervous. When I panic, my heart feels weak and pumps more blood than it should, so they called my father to calm me down.

Five minutes later, I found him in front of me with red cheeks and eyes sticking out of their sockets.

"Holy shit, Tobia, is it possible that you always cause trouble? You screwed up my day!" he said, trying to take my hand.

But I wriggled and, without waiting for him, I headed for the car.

"I want to go home. I want to get out of this shitty school!"

I realized that my father was also furious. I didn't want to make him angry, but it was done. When Mom opened the door, she was holding a kitchen towel in her hand and carefully polishing a plate; she was still in her dressing gown. The TV was blaring in the living room, while a couple was doing their best in a dance that seemed to me to be a tango.

"Tobia, why so soon?" she blurted, amazed.

"I kicked and the door got a hole in it..." I answered, confessing only part of my reaction.

The plate slipped from her hands, and as it hit the floor, it shattered into a thousand pieces.

"It's-all-the-fault-of-that-ring..." I replied, stammering.

Then, I went up to my room and picked up Brilly and Loly from under the bed. As I waited for them to stick their heads out of the carapace and bite into the salad I had hidden under my pillow, I thought that my parents were one-star people!

A Night Full
of Nightmares

– CHAPTER 12 –

I decided I would no longer go to school, but it was not meant to be.

I felt distressed and not happy at all. I was not at peace with myself because no one believed I was an innocent boy — specifically that I was not a thief. How that ring ended up in my man purse, I just can't explain.

As a matter of principle, my mother, who demands good manners, taught me that I should not take objects that do not belong to me, even though I love to collect small items that I find around my house to place in my man purse. When you give me precise orders, I am strict about following them.

But in the world, there are honest people and dishonest people. Well, the latter, as my father says, are capable of doing anything, even stealing. And someone, rather dishonest, had robbed Mrs. Cristina and then placed the stolen goods in my man purse.

"Because of this theft, not everyone considers me an honest boy!" I said to my father.

And he answered without mincing words:

"Tell me who doubts your innocence and, I swear, I'll break their faces!"

"Those two particular carabinieri," I replied, looking at his sweater with a large oil stain on its belly.

"Holy shit, Tobia, they found it in your man purse, that ring!" he replied sorrowfully, realizing that he could not break the snouts of the two carabinieri. "Is it possible that you don't know how it ended up there? From now on, please stay out of trouble!" he concluded, scratching his head.

That night I had nightmares, and the next day, I remained in bed. In fact, I stayed in bed for many more days. I felt sick and needed peace. Everything bothered me, even the ringing of the phone. I hated the persistent noise, as if it were announcing another trouble for me.

I believe this story contributed to my depression. That is, I lost the desire to get up, wash, go to school, and even eat. I was no longer following my roadmap.

My mother had a lot to do to convince me to care for myself. So, one day, she took me by force and dragged me to the bathroom; then, with a push, she placed me under the hot shower, making me risk being boiled to death.

She soaped me up with a chamomile bubble bath and rubbed my skin so hard that, in the end, I became a cloud of fragrant foam. Like Dominique, she is also a fan of the language of flowers and believes that the chamomile fragrance provides strength in times of difficulty. Finally, she rinsed me with a jet of hot water.

I yelled as much as I could, then I gave up.

With this push and pull, two weeks passed by.

My special needs teacher came home several times to convince me to resume lessons. He told me about the play that had been left pending and that I cared about very much. He talked about the friends who were looking for me and my desk, which was always empty. But I, faithful to my oath, was always found in bed, and I even resumed peeing in my underwear.

One day, Dominique arrived unexpectedly. He had gel-soaked hair, wore boots cut at the top to accommodate his thick calves, a pair of skinny jeans, and a trendy jacket that smelled of the usual lavender.

His fixation on flowers has worsened since reading Vanessa Diffenbaugh's book "The Secret Language of Flowers," prompting him to go to great lengths to prove that their healing power is valid in every field.

He is convinced that the aroma of lavender helps regain confidence. Conversely, in my opinion, he is also very obtuse because he pretends not to understand that, for quite some time, I no longer like flowers because they remind me of Mrs. Cristina.

Nevertheless, he insisted:

"Come to school, Tobia. I brought the guitar, and with your friend Pier Luigi, we decided to play. We need someone who knows all the songs of the Eighties, and only you know them. And then... guess what?... I have something for you! I have a letter that your schoolmates wrote."

But I didn't want to read it. Then, Dominique cleared his throat and read:

Dear Tobia,

We miss you very much. Without you, the classroom feels empty to us. We miss your jokes and your liveliness. You are a special friend to us, and every day, when we see your empty seat, we feel sad. We all believe in your innocence, and you will see that everything will become clear.

We are waiting for you – with love.

Your classmates

"I'm so confused because those damn chicks are cackling a lot in my head," I replied, instead.

"They say peep, Tobia, peep. Can't you really fight them?" he urged, as he tried to convince me to get up.

"No. I can't get rid of them... They make me anxious about that ring thing."

"Okay. Okay," he answered, caressing me. "We all know you're not guilty, champ. But now get up; they are waiting for you at school. Unfortunately, sometimes, episodes happen that make us feel bad and sad, but then everything is fixed. You will see, everything will be cleared up, as your classmates wrote. Do you understand, Tobia?"

"Why-is-life-so-complicated?" I said, seeking his help.

"Come on, these difficult times will pass, and you will return to being a happy boy," he specified.

That was definitely a day so and so.

Dominique says depression is not good for you, so you must fight it. Even if the nightmares and anger have passed, the daze and sluggishness from that extended stay in bed still linger.

So, convinced by his reasoning, I got dressed. I took off my pajamas and put on my underwear, T-shirt, and pants. I thought I was in order when Dominique rebuked me:

"How did you dress, Tobia!"

I looked at my outfit and saw that I had worn my underwear backwards, my shirt inside out, and my brother's pants!

But that Monday, a day with even letters, was a good time to start again, even if I felt so messed up. And then, as my mother used to say, there was always time to die!

With my Friend, Pilù

I don't remember if I've said it before, but I'm not easy at friend-ships. It is not easy for me to be with others because those who are with me need a good dose of patience.

Usually, I don't like to talk. and when I do, I follow a logic of my own that does not always coincide with the thoughts of others. More-over, when I listen to others, I go by the association of words, remain silent, or talk about things that have nothing to do with the discourse in progress.

Let me give some examples.

The other day, someone said the word "ring." Hearing that term was enough for me to lose my patience, and, without realizing it, I found myself on the ground beating my classmate as hard as I could. Yet, there was no connection with the theft of Mrs. Cristina's ring. Loris had simply said that he had given a ring to his girlfriend.

Another problem is that I don't know how to associate words that are the same but have different meanings: when someone says the word "rose," I think of the lady who lives in the same building as my house and not, perhaps, the flower that is also a rose.

Moreover, I don't like to be touched, and it doesn't take much for trouble to arise. I remember that time when Benedetta, upon see-ing me, embraced me with exaggerated affection: I reacted strongly because she held me, and I didn't like it at all. I pushed her away so forcefully that the poor girl fell and fractured her ankle.

But with Pilù, it is different. I love him, even if I never tell him. He is a special guy.

My friend Pilù follows me like a shadow and is a smart guy. He doesn't touch me or squeeze me, and he carefully listens to my speeches, which others define as weird. Very often, at school, he keeps me company when Dominique arrives late or is busy drafting the minutes of the class council.

With Pilù, I traveled every day along the road that leads to school, and always with him, I stopped at Mrs. Cristina's to have fun with the parrot Chicorita. However, since the day of the theft, I have no longer done this.

Pilù knows everything about parrots. One day, he told me that he dreams of a holiday in Australia, where the Loriidae live. He would like to raise them and train them to speak.

Lorikeets are small to medium-sized parrots, about the size of two fists. They have sturdy legs and are quite amusing animals with spray-like droppings. Their brightly colored plumage features a pointed or bristled tongue adapted for feeding on nectar, pollen, and soft, juicy fruits. Their wings are tapered, and their tails are pointed. Pilù clarifies that this enables them to fly with agility.

My father, on the other hand, says that to see these specimens, you don't necessarily have to go to Australia. Simply buy a book on the subject, and you can learn all about parrots. Many people go on holiday to Australia to see parrots, but they don't realize they can study them in specialized ornithology books.

The word comes from the Greek ὄρνις, òrnis, meaning "bird." It is a branch of zoology that studies the class of birds. However, Dominique told me this during science class.

Pilù isn't interested in all of this. He enjoys traveling and mentioned that he will travel to Australia when he gets older because he doesn't trust advertising photos or books in general.

Pilù is the only friend I truly cherish. We discovered that we share the same birthday. He is very kind, with a face full of freckles and perpetually tousled blond hair. He mentions that he strives to be neat whenever he can, just to present himself with a sense of composure.

He enjoys chewing gum and stuffs a great deal of it into his mouth, risking the possibility of sounding like a real idiot, chewing it like a cow before blowing big balloons. Then, he pinches them with his fingers and pulls a long, rubbery thread that he twists around his tongue, causing me to laugh a lot.

The other day, while I was at school, I found myself in front of him with his stepmother, who, seeing me, came toward me like a chicken. Her nose was as pointed as an owl's beak, and her two small eyes looked at me through the lenses of her glasses.

She was constantly agitated, just as I am when I am anxious, and, grabbing me with her fat hands, she blew a kiss on my cheek, just before I could escape her affectionate nonsense.

"What a darling boy!" she said, walking backwards, when I clapped my hands in anger because her kiss had terrified me.

"I think, however, that this friend of yours is confounded!" she noted afterward, turning to Pilù, with her false teeth that moved when speaking.

Finally, irritated by my behavior and fidgeting in her old dress adorned with large peony flower prints, she walked away from me.

Mala Tempora Currunt!

— CHAPTER 14 —

Every now and then, my mother launches into quotes just to give herself a tone.

She says that there is nothing strange and that she learned Latin at school. When she is angry, once in a while, she nails us with a complaint, which is almost always a quote of sorts. She explained that the proverbs are truths derived from experience, and the Latin ones are the most famous.

The last one I heard her pronounce, in chronological order, is "mala tempora currunt," used when you want to affirm that bad times are current, and that is: we are going through a bad time.

It's a Latin phrase, she says, but I don't understand Latin.

My father, on the other hand, who is much more practical, doesn't go for subtlety; he says that when it rains, it pours, because that fucking ring is driving him crazy. The other day, for example, he made me sit in the living room of the house, where it is forbidden to play, and, measuring his words, he said to me:

"You know, Tobia, we have to talk. Know that I believe you, but you must explain the story of the ring to me in detail."

"I know that!" I thought. But what I knew vanished from my mind just as I was about to open my mouth. I felt total emptiness in my brain, as if a deep black hole had swallowed all my words. As he spoke, my attention fixated on the vein in his neck that was swelling and on his voice that, to my ears, was shrill and lamenting.

"You're sure you didn't get that ring, Tobia? So, perhaps, by mistake?"

Not satisfied, he continued: "Because, if so, everything will be fixed."

"No, I didn't take it," I replied with all sincerity.

"Well," he yelled, "if it wasn't you, how the fuck did it get into your man purse?"

"I don't know," I stammered, as I ate the olives.

"You know," he said again, "we have decided to take you to an Institute."

"Do you really want to do that?" I asked, swallowing more olives with all the pits.

"Of course, it is a Residential Institute. You will stay there even at night, but we will come to visit you every Sunday," he replied, trying to sweeten the pill.

I noticed that the vein in his neck began to swell even more, indicating that his patience was running out. My father is an *impulsive man.* My mother always says it when she scolds him: "Calm down, dear, don't be impulsive," she says. So, I didn't worry.

"You're-telling-me-that-you-send-me-away,-because-they-say-I-stole-the-ring-of-lady-Cristina? But-I-didn't-steal-that-ring," I said, stammering even louder, as I continued to stare at his neck.

My father held my face in his hands and compelled me to look into his eyes, as the vein throbbed dangerously, growing bluer and bluer.

"But no. Theft has nothing to do with it," he said with the air of someone who had been caught stealing jam directly from the jar. "It's just to give you back serenity and greater humoral balance... and then they said that you will have to take psycho-aptitude tests... Every now and then, there are those tests, and to do that, you must go to a center... that is, in an Institute... In short, in a suitable place, you know..." he stammered, trying not to go haywire and finally letting go of my face.

At that point, I had to ask him what the terms "tests" and "psycho-aptitudes" meant. He looked at me, wrinkling his nose, then faltered:

"We need... need... they are being used to understand your level of intelligence, your relationships and your emotions, and many other things... You know, I had to do them a long time ago too, to see if I was fit for the job. But you don't have to worry because in this institute you will learn new things and... and..."

"But-I-already attend my-eeemhm-Professional-Institute-for-the-Crafts," I hesitated, slowly elaborating my thought.

"Holy shit, Tobia. Why do you make everything more difficult? That school is no longer for you; you must learn to do something else."

At that point, his vein beat rhythmically, and it seemed he no longer wanted to stop: my father had completely lost his patience.

Teacher Giacomina, once, when I was a child, told me that I was a lucky boy because my parents loved me, and that everyone loved me. Then, with the finger paint, she wrote on a piece of paper: "Tobia is good, and we love him."

I felt uncertain. If my parents had chosen to send me to an institute, it meant they no longer loved me.

I didn't know what a residential institute was, since I had never been there. So, I thought it wouldn't be nice to leave home.

When I was younger, my parents avoided sending me to an institute by calling the teacher Giacomina to teach me many things, including reading and writing, because my hand was unable to hold a pen or any other object. Additionally, I was cross-eyed, and my eyes looked in completely different directions. Together, we established a work plan tailored to the circumstances, proceeding with specific goals.

Goal 1: Grab and squeeze things.
Goal 2: Rotate your wrist while grasping the object.
Goal 3: Hold the grip and then let go to place the object in the right place.
Goal 4: Coordinate the use of both hands.

Goal 5: Force the eye to look in a precise direction.

Goal 6: Coordinate your eyes and look at the face of any person.

"An exercise aimed at activating the fine motor skills for the correct use of the hands and, of course, of the fingers, wrist, and eyes," said Giacomina in the end, trying to explain that torture to me.

Well, maybe it was time to learn new things in a context other than home. So, my parents decided to send me to that institute, but I didn't want to go. Instead, I wanted clarity about the ring, so I decided to run away from home.

My Highlight

My parents had decided everything without consulting me. No one thought that my opinion was important. So, I didn't have a way to escape as I had planned.

One morning, after washing and applying perfume, we got dressed. Then, we dragged a suitcase that was inflated like a balloon into the car and left for what my father called "a trip".

Instead, they took me to a special institute.

"You'll see, Tobia, you'll like it!" he said in a cheerful voice.

Maybe I acted foolishly because I didn't anticipate where we were headed. However, I can't foresee the future. I prefer to live in the present and rarely consider that tomorrow might differ from today. I am someone who does not abandon habits, even if others label them as stereotypies.

For example, I always get up at the same time in the morning and wear the same clothes. Unless my mom manages to carry out a raid once a week, replacing my dirty laundry with clean ones. Sometimes, making her desperate, I decide to do precisely the opposite: I wash and change my clothes all the time.

I always have breakfast with cinnamon soy milk and the usual biscuits, always four in number. When Mom happens to put out five, because she is distracted, I take the fifth cookie and put it back in the box because an odd number brings me bad luck.

With a certain rigor, I brush my teeth. To tell the truth, I chew on the toothbrush to the point that the bristles are all badly tilted outwards.

Before going to school, I pass by my room. I fight with my brother, and, with a very specific gesture, I unmake the bed that my mother has just made. Then, I pick up the man purse while my father punctually shouts:

"Tobia, do you want to move? You're late!"

My father doesn't accompany me to school because I can go a-lone. It is part of the program provided by group H, which stands for Handicap and is part of the autonomy discourse. This means I always walk the same street to school: five straight blocks before reaching the building. However, I walk six to avoid the odd number. The sixth block is where Mrs. Cristina lives, on the ground floor of an old building with eight rather shabby apartments. There are actually seven, but I always count eight.

I think Mrs. Cristina acts as a doorman because she always comes out of a glass cage overlooking the exit, which also has a small garden. Outside the door, also made of glass, she usually puts Chicorita, her parrot. It is there that I met my friend Pilù and other boys in my class until that infamous day of the ring theft.

When I get home, the first thing I do is lower all the shutters and turn on the light, even when the sun is shining. This makes my parents very angry because they don't like artificial light in broad daylight; as a result, we start arguing. Then, I turn on the radio. I know all the songs from the Seventies and Eighties by heart, and this amuses me because they broadcast the same music every day. My mother explained to me that these are recorded programs, where they always play the same things. This comforts me because I am not the only one who is so methodical — that is, so obsessed.

Afterward, during the afternoon, even in winter, I go to bed in the sense that I lie down. Sometimes, my parents have engagements, and must take me with them, so they are in a hurry. But I don't give up;

I don't skip this ritual at all: I undress, lie down, and afterward, get up and get dressed within ten minutes.

In the afternoon, my teacher Giacomina comes to give me private lessons. We study a bit of geography, especially about Australia, where my friend Pilù would like to go. I learned that Australia is a large island located between the Indian Ocean and the Pacific Ocean, which is not very peaceful because there are often floods and earthquakes.

I'm very good at calculations. However, my strong point is addition, such as two plus two, which makes four. I dislike two plus three because it results in five, along with all the other numbers that yield an odd sum. Therefore, we have fun eliminating all the odd numbers, which is not easy. I can also manage multiplication. I know the multiplication table well because, with it, you can never go wrong.

The school psychologist once asked me why I preferred even numbers over odd numbers. I replied that I liked them because they made me feel safer. Additionally, no number was left alone since they were always divisible by two.

Dinnertime is a moment I enjoy because it signals the end of the day. When I'm tired, I don't watch TV; instead, I prefer to wash up and go to bed. Even if these are stereotypes, as others say, I feel calm because I know the next day will be very similar to the previous one, and the teacher Giacomina, who has lately also been wearing a nice bra, as I have noticed, will return again.

But the morning we left, polished to the nines and getting into the car, I had a feeling that I would have to stop practicing all those good habits of mine and that our trip would not be pleasant; while Lucio Battisti sang on the radio Fiori rosa, Fiori di pesco (Pink flowers, Peach flowers), I found myself thinking like Dominique.

According to the language of flowers, the peach tree represents immense love, and I felt overwhelmed by the suffocating love of my parents.

The Garden of Happy Children

– CHAPTER 16 –

The car took an avenue lined with oleanders. The flowers, first white, then pink, and finally red, paraded before my eyes like colored waves, so much so that I felt seasick; so much so that Dominique's voice buzzed in my ears saying:

"Tobia, be careful; you must be wary of this plant because it is poisonous!"

He always mentioned this during gardening hours to curb my habit of cutting all the flowers I encountered in my path.

On the other hand, the building was enclosed by a rather high boundary wall with a gigantic sign reading "The garden of the happy boys." It housed a series of workshops of various kinds: a carpentry shop, a glass factory, a gym, and many other rooms with different activities. A small chapel offered a glimpse of many flowers and a Christ hanging from a wooden cross. He was very distressed and full of wounds, which impressed me.

In the center, a large window and a grand staircase led to the upper floors, where the various apartments were located. One of these had been assigned to me. I counted the floors that comprised the building and found three of them. This seemed inconsistent, so I imagined a fourth floor. I was very nervous because my parents were speaking with the Educator. Then I saw my mother crying. Surely, they were discussing me, and to manage my anxiety, I touched my man purse filled with all my little things, and then I took Brilly and Loly out of the box.

I keep my turtles in a tin box since they are as big as half a fist. I gave them a piece of lettuce that had rotted a little by keeping it too long in my pocket. Despite all this, I could not be serene.

To Mr. Martino, who welcomed me first and whom my father described as tall and rigid as a stick, I explained that I was there because of a theft, but I was not a thief.

Mom always says that when you meet a new person, it's good to clarify your position to avoid misunderstandings. So, I tried to figure out whether Mr. Martino was my friend or my enemy.

"What kind of theft, Tobia?" asked the educator in his gentle voice.

"The theft of Mrs. Cristina's ring! The carabinieri found it in my man purse, but I don't know how it ended there. I'm also angry because since that day, everyone turns to me every time an object goes missing at school."

"I'm sorry, Tobia. I also believe that it wasn't you who carried out the theft, even if your mania for collecting items falls under those unintentional thefts called kleptomania. In short, you feel attracted to everything you like, but it's not your fault. It is a neurotic symptom— an irrepressible and unmotivated need to steal. It is that desire to take possession of objects, even without value. But don't worry, it's a disease that can be cured..."

It was then that I finally understood the meaning of that difficult word. I was a kleptomaniac, which in simple terms meant thief, even if involuntary, and no one had explained it to me!

"Is that why my parents left me here?" I asked, aware that I wasn't a real thief.

"You see, Tobia, by law, you are the only one who carried out the theft. The stolen goods, moreover, were in your man purse, and this indicates that you are the only culprit. Your parents have brought you here so that you can find peace of mind with the help of experienced people.

It is a concrete way to improve your quality of life through therapeutic activities... In short, you are here to treat yourself, so rest assured..."

"I'm already a quiet guy... And then, I don't like being here, even if everything is in order and there are also horses."

"Ah, have you seen the racetrack? Do you like it? You know, we practice hippotherapy. The horses are very tame, and the boys relax and become attached to the animals as well."

I've always liked horses. I saw some of them because I have a friend who owns fields and horses in the country. An acquaintance of mine brings there his son, who can't stand up and, when he speaks, he drools all over. I tried to ride one, but I gave up. I still haven't gotten used to it," I said, looking at the sharp tip of his red pencil as he wrote on the paper notes.

"Do you mind telling me the story of the ring, Tobia?" said the man, pointing at me with two inquiring eyes that I interpreted as accusatory.

I gazed at the tip of his pencil for a long time before answering. I sensed that my guilt or innocence would derive from that point.

Like in a movie, I relived that damn day again, so I began to tell the story, searching my brain for the right words. I told Mr. Martino how the facts unfolded because I have an infallible memory. My brain is like a camera, and when I want to, I let the scenes flow as if I were reliving them.

But suddenly, Mr. Martino asked me a trick question.

"While you were playing with the parrot, how did you manage to remove the ring from Mrs. Cristina's finger?"

At a certain point, I remembered that Mrs. Cristina did not have the ring on her finger. Instead, it sparkled on the shelf of the parrot's cage. After a few minutes, it disappeared.

"What's the matter, Tobia, do you have difficulty remembering?"

"No. It's that the ring was resting on the shelf of the cage."

"If you remember exactly where it was, tell me: did you take it?!"

It felt like receiving a blow to the head. I realized that Mr. Martino was definitely my enemy.

I took my head in my hands to avoid the chicks that were coming, and I felt the blood throbbing in my ears, chest, and temples, with my heart beating very fast. Then, I also felt that my stomach was about to explode, just like when I drink cow's milk by mistake, I get a big stomachache and am forced to run to the bathroom. But before I knew it, I threw up on myself and on Mr. Martino's desk as well, just like what happened in Porretta when I threw up on the table.

When I calmed down, I found myself in my room, sucking my thumb — a long-standing habit that has made it long and thin. Yet, I was happy all the same because those little animals were gone, and I was wearing new clothing that smelled of lavender. I looked around, thinking about my teacher Dominique, and saw only a tall, thin boy trying to smile at me. He had a deck of cards in his hands, and in an attempt to greet me, he tossed me an eight of diamonds. It was an even card, which made me like him.

Tommy

I listened to Tommy's breathing and counted the irregular exhalations and inhalations: one–two, one–two, one–two, one–two. I noticed that Tommy always blew a whistle at the two. And always at the two, I ended up putting my hands to my ears because I couldn't stand that hiss. Additionally, when he spoke, he stammered — a disorder that made him resemble me when I was nervous.

They explained to me that Tommy would be my roommate and that he was asthmatic, so, when he breathed, he made a loud whistle. He was very good at playing cards and, for this reason, I had to be careful not to challenge him, as I would undoubtedly lose. He also had the habit of expressing his sympathies through cards. The higher the card, the more sympathy he felt for the person he became fond of. On the other hand, he signaled with a two of Spades the people he disliked.

When he was not playing with cards, he was at the computer. He had his own email and wrote very long letters to his friends. I envied his skill and all those friendships for a while. Then, one day, Tommy told me that the letters he wrote were called emails and that the people he sent them to were not real but lived in his imagination, and that he had a lot of fun always inventing new ones. He specified that I was the first real person not born from his brain, and therefore, I was not his friend, so I had to be very careful not to meddle in his games.

Teacher Giacomina always told me that games can be competitive, and in this case, only the best win. Cooperation, on the other hand, fosters relationships of mutual help: a type of competitive game immediately emerged between Tommy and me.

In the first few days, we looked at each other with suspicion, being careful not to touch. He played continuously with his cards, engaging in an endless solitaire game that sometimes lasted whole days. He arranged the cards precisely, and no one had to interfere.

"To-to-Tobia, do not to-to-touch my ca-cards, a-a-otherwise, you're f-f-fried!" he would say, sputtering like a machine gun.

I, on the other hand, set out to define the spaces that belonged to me with the toys I took out of my bag and scattered everywhere, just to mark my territory.

Under the bed, I put the box with Brilly and Loly, and when I went to lunch, I took care to take some salad from my companion for my turtles.

We continued like this for about a month. In short, we thoroughly studied each other to catch the first culprit who would invade the life of the other.

Then, one day, Tommy's breath stopped. I thought he was going to die. His face turned purple, and he peed for a long time. I was scared to death because I didn't know what to do in that situation. Then I remembered that my mother often trained my siblings to call for help when I had epileptic seizures and got wet. So, I started banging loudly on the desk I shared with my friend. Finally, the educator came and took Tommy away to save him from that crisis.

The next day, Tommy resumed his life in our room.

"Hello!" I said as soon as I entered. I was returning from the carpentry workshop, where I had collected many shavings to put in Brilly and Loly's boxes in anticipation of their hibernation.

Instead of greeting me, Tommy looked at me and threw me a playing card that fell upside down; I bent down and took it in my hands: it was a ten of Diamonds.

"Well", I thought, "he likes me".

Then, I returned the card to him, took a string from the bedside table, and said:

"Take it. You can keep it, if you want."

Tommy pretended nothing had happened and, ignoring my disappointment, said:

"T-t-they're yours, t-t-those?"

"You mean Brilly and Loly?" I replied.

"Yes, t-t--those t-t-t-turtles".

He said those words with a certain breathlessness and whistled with every breath.

"Brilly is a very peaceful and clean beast, as is her twin sister Loly. They are called that because I like names that end with a "y." Soon, they will go into hibernation, so I am building the den for them".

"G-g-good". Then, after a long silence, he continued: "H-how come you e-ended up here?"

"There's only one reason I'm here: they say I stole a ring from a lady who has a parrot."

"T-they say, or did you s-steal it f-for real?"

I was left thinking; the situation was getting out of hand. My father recommends that I reflect before answering because our lives also depend on our words.

"No. I didn't steal it, even if they say I'm a kleptomaniac. But the carabinieri, during a search, found it in my man purse ..."

"N-not n-n-necessarily a k-kleptomaniac is a t-thief, my friend. T-those who suffer from this mania are f-forced to t-take o-objects because they are driven by a s-strong impulse. But you are not a r-real thief! Whoever s-stole it, i-instead, put it in your m-man purse, really and of course, that is not you," replied Tommy, with his usual stammer.

"How do you know?" I asked, amazed by such intuition and above all, grateful for having been cleared of that accusation.

"It's l-logical, isn't it?" he said, shuffling the cards.

"And why is it so logical? Why would he put it in my man purse?" I replied, waiting for his answer.

"S-simple. The t-thief is a f-friend of yours who was about to be d-discovered and having a chance, he e-exploited it. He felt unsafe and, unaware of your p-problem, hid it in your m-man purse. So, if the c-carabinieri hadn't searched you, he would have taken back the ring, g-getting away with it. But it was unlucky, because the c-c-carabinieri also rummaged through your m-man purse and..."

"Yes, but I was also unlucky because they accused me."

"And you have never thought of l-looking for the real c-culprit? You know, it's a question of j-justice!"

"I've never engaged in this because I'm not a cop or an investigator..."

"Oh, my God To-Tobia, you must get away from here. You absolutely have to find the real c-culprit, if you want to prove your innocence!"

At that moment, I remembered the book I had read with Giacomina some time ago: Christopher, the protagonist, had become an investigator to solve the case of the dog killed at midnight. Therefore, I deduced that I could follow his example by investigating my case.

As I pondered this, a girl entered the room holding a stuffed cat and wearing a daisy in her hair.

"E-cco," said Tommy, "Madame F-Fantasy has arrived, s-simple and p-pure as a f-flower," and, saying this, he gave her a long bow. Then he threw her the ten of diamonds, which meant he was in love with her.

Madame Fantasy is a Fantasy

– CHAPTER 18 –

Madame Fantasy, like Tommy, ended with the letter 'y,' and for this reason alone, I liked it immediately. However, just like for Tommy, Fantasy was also a name composed of an odd number of letters, which was not favorable according to my theory.

I decided, however, that I would make an exception for the two of them.

Teacher Giacomina always said that "the exception proves the rule." In this way, I reserved my sympathy for my two friends while maintaining a particular reservation for unusual words.

It was forbidden to pronounce her real name, so Tommy had renamed her *Fantasy*.

The girl smiled at me. Then, she began to hum several words, such as "mom," "radar," "refer," "rotator," and "pup," while she twisted the cat's tail around her finger.

"Don't worry," Tommy told me, with the usual asthmatic whistle marking his every word, "it's always like this when she meets a new b-buddy. Her s-schizophrenia makes her live in a world all her own. Sometimes, she acts like an g-ghost, other times she plays pranks, but she always smiles. After all, she's g-good and she's also b-beautiful, don't you think?"

Then it occurred to me that I should say something because Tommy's question needed a response. And questions, as my mother says, must always be answered. It is good manners, she specifies.

"She's beautiful," I said. "But I don't like the daisy in her hair." Then I added, "Even my neighbor sometimes acts like a ghost. Last Halloween, she dressed in a long white sheet and came to visit us to play a joke on us. Mom then said, 'Oh my God, Tobia, this is the ghost of Mrs. Lucy.'

It was funny to me for three reasons: first, because the word ghost was even in number; second, because Lucy ended with a *y*; third, that her name was also made up of even letters.

I kept my eyes fixed on Madame Fantasy because, apart from that ridiculous flower on her head, she reminded me of a nineteenth-century girl that Dominique had shown me in history books. She was just like her, blonde with bobbed hair and skin the color of the golden moon. She wore an ankle-length cream dress with dirt stains scattered all over and walked barefoot.

I wanted to say something to her, but nothing came to mind. Then I heard my own voice saying, "***Racecar, solos, noon.***" I felt my face ablaze. But by now it was done because, in that way, I had entered her world. She smiled at me and sent me kisses, curling her mouth like a chicken's ass while pooing, as Tommy said.

The palindromic words had been taught to me by my friend Pilù, when we went to Mrs. Cristina's to have fun with her parrot. They can be read from left to right and from right to left.

In addition, Dominique, considering my interest in the subject, had also wanted to teach me about the syllabic palindrome, which derives from Greek and means "that runs backwards."

They were exercises that amused me a lot, so I tried to find some words, such as: ***gaga, mama, papa***. Except that these words can be read two by two, going from right to left.

Then, I remembered another palindrome word and suddenly said "***Anna.***"

Madame Fantasy pounced on me unceremoniously and beat me to death. Without realizing it, I had pronounced her name, which irritated her: I had unknowingly uncovered her secret.

Tommy tried to help me, but Anna's fury was beyond our strength, so, giving up, he said:

"A-a-anna, f-fuck you!" At that, she stopped and left.

The next day, the Director told me that he was very sorry for what had happened to me, but the girl sometimes reacted violently when she heard her real name pronounced. Her schizophrenia was a mental disorder that interfered with her ability to think.

I, too, am sometimes impulsive, but there is always my father who scolds me.

"Fuck, Tobia, think before you answer. Count to at least ten!"

The director insisted that I disinfect the wounds with iodine tincture and apply bandages to my right arm and leg.

From that day on, I no longer looked Anna in the face and kept away from her. However, this was not enough to prevent Madame Fantasy from beating me again. I can't stand it when someone hits me for no reason.

I had to do something; I couldn't take any more risks. So, I decided to follow Tommy's advice. I had to flee and return home for two important reasons: first, because I couldn't stand Madame Fantasy anymore; second, because I needed to find the real thief of the ring. To console myself, I stuck my thumb in my mouth...

My Escape

I had never seen the sea, so I decided to head to a town on the coast, and Bari was the closest one. I took the man purse and filled it with all my objects: the red screwdriver, the green one, shoelaces, two clothespins, a colored rubber ball, a red car, a black one, two yellow ones without wheels, ten phone cards, a photo of my brothers, a crumb of hard bread, a paper clip, four strips of paper stuck to it by a melted candy, and many other things. To the man purse, I also added the box with Brilly and Loly; I couldn't leave without taking them, as they were my turtles.

I put my hands in my pockets and found some euros. I had no idea how much money I would need, nor how long I would be away before returning home. I thought that perhaps I would not even be able to find my way home: I had never traveled alone, and this scared me. Mom said there were a lot of bad people around, but that's only partially true. I still had to be on the lookout and not trust strangers.

As I got dressed, I heard one of my companions in the next room snoring and another tugging at him to make him stop. Then I heard the footsteps of the educator, busy upstairs with a boy who peed on himself, wetting his bed. Madame Fantasy, fortunately, slept soundly in the women's ward...

Before leaving, I peeped through the keyhole to make sure everyone was asleep. Then, I called Tommy, who helped me escape.

At that time, several trains were leaving for the city of Bari. Trains have always intrigued me; at home, I have a model that I tore to pieces. However, what I was about to take was a real train, and it was huge and made entirely of iron. I chose one that was multicolored, with the side writing — Freight train —.

Tommy had told me that to travel by train, you needed a ticket, which I didn't have. Therefore, the freight train seemed ideal for traveling illegally because it was carrying goods and not people, and this way, I would not have to explain to anyone why I was fleeing. It was Tommy who had suggested this trick to me, and it seemed like a good idea to me.

But "freight train" was two odd words, so I stopped abruptly and studied the situation for a while. I combined the two words and tried to separate the consonants from the vowels. I always do this before joining the letters and forming the word in full. I discovered that there were four vowels and eight consonants: two even numbers. At this point I understood that everything would be fine, which gave me the courage to continue my escape.

Tommy looked at me, puzzled, and then said:

"D-don't you feel like you're exaggerating with the s-story of even n-numbers?"

So, I explained to him that it was not much different from how he behaved with his cards, indicating to people whether he liked them or not.

And once again, I explained to him that I like even numbers because there are no leftovers and that everything is fine. Then, I added:

There are five of us in my house, and this is not good. If I do the math, my parents are two and they are together; my brothers are two and they are together, while I am the odd one out and always alone.

But Tommy pointed out that my speech was not logical and that mine was simply a family; families are always together, whether odd or even. What mattered was loving each other.

"But I," I specified clarifying my ideas, "I have not been in the family for a long time! Now I don't know if my family still loves me, since I was accused of theft and my parents took me to this *educational institute*, with the excuse that I need to recover. I cannot escape my fate!"

"Which d-destiny, T-Tobia?"

"To survive!" I replied bitterly.

"I'm sorry," said my friend. "I'm very sorry also because you're leaving. If you want, I c-can c-come with you. T-t-together, the ca-ca-rabinieri will not find us. I know that it wasn't you who s-stole the ring of Mrs. Cristina."

"Never mind," I said, "you must help Madame Fantasy, and I must find who stole the ring. That's why I run away; I can't stand to be accused of faults I don't have!"

"Y-you know, at least, where y-you're going?" he asked me worriedly.

Well, I haven't thought about it yet. I'll go somewhere; Bari is a big city. At most, I might go home.

"If you change your mind, you can always come back to me," he continued, his voice asthmatic. Then, my friend approached me and hugged me. I didn't move.

"W-well, g-good l-luck," he said. And before turning to leave, he threw me four cards: a ten of Clubs, a one of Spades, a one of Hearts, and a one of Diamonds.

I stood there for a long time until Tommy turned the corner and I couldn't see him anymore. I was left with his asthmatic breath in my ears and his smell to keep me company. By now, I had become accustomed to his breathing and the odor of stagnant piss on his pants. This reminded me of my father's words:

"Tobia, holy... don't wet yourself anymore. You're grown up now!"

I had never felt my heart beating so fast. My teacher Giacomina says that my heart is as big as a fist and that, being a muscle, it can be strong or weak. It's strong when I run, laugh, and I'm happy; it's weak when I cry, stand still, or I'm sad. Blood circulates through the tubes called arteries and veins, which I feel pulsing and bursting in my chest when I am agitated or sad.

Well, at that moment I felt sad, very sad. I looked out of the train window, and the country was now far, far away.

Bari Station

– CHAPTER 20 –

As soon as I got off the train, I encountered a young man walking along the sidewalk, kicking a can that he sent flying a few seconds later, and a lady with a budgie, begging. Even though it wasn't Mrs. Cristina, I kept my distance from her.

City stations differ significantly from village stations. I mention this because, once, my teacher Giacomina took me for a walk to the outskirts of my town, where we came across a rectangular house painted brick red.

There was a sign that read "TICKET OFFICE." I liked the two words immediately because they had an even number of letters. Beyond the entrance, after a sidewalk, two parallel iron bars of infinite length called tracks extended.

I thought about the binary number system that the math professor had explained one day, which uses two symbols: 0 and 1. It is an abstract concept because mathematics itself is a notion that cannot be understood without a clear enough framework in mind. However, it's too complicated for me to explain since it's not my area of expertise.

At that moment, a train arrived and emitted a whistle so loud that it made me plug my ears. I can't stand loud noises; they penetrate my head and make me lose concentration. My teacher informed me that this place was called a station, where trains passed through, and people went there to travel to other places. They are a necessary means of moving from one place to another. The train's whistle is like a call of love for those returning home and a great call of pain for those who leave forever.

The station in the city of Bari, which was much more spacious than the other one, was crowded with a large number of people walking in two directions: those who arrived and those who departed. People branched off busily toward the streets filled with cars that made loud noises with the roar of their engines.

This time, I also plugged my ears.

I felt very confused, and to avoid getting lost, I crouched on the ground and took the tin box with Brilly and Loly out of my pocket. Then, I opened my man purse. The playing cards that Tommy had given me and sixty euros in tens, which my father had given me for my initial needs at the Institute, came out. It was then that I remembered I had escaped from the center with the strange name "The Garden of Happy Children," where my parents had left me.

I wandered around for days. I had never felt so free to do what I wanted. The trouble was, however, that I didn't know what decision to make. So, I gave myself a schedule, just like teacher Giacomina did when I wandered around aimlessly during the day. I decided, therefore, to:

1°: Inspect the area where I was.
2°: Look for a place to eat and drink. (Because I eat and drink a lot).
3°: Look for a place to sleep.
4°: Try not to spend a lot of money.

My parents, along with my teachers, taught me that you must always know where you are. This is called spatial orientation. I excel at this because, even if I don't show it, I can navigate alone in an unfamiliar place. Once, I was able to drive around my entire village by myself and memorize all the road signs I encountered on the streets.

This earned me praise from the school principal, who used me as an example for the entire school.

Another necessity for humans is providing food to avoid dying of hunger. Besides spaghetti, I love eating oranges, Oreos with chocolate, and fries. So, I decided I would only eat those. Then I remembered that I enjoy drinking Coca-Cola, but maybe I would have given that up because my mother says it swells my stomach and makes me burp indecently.

If I had managed to spend one euro a day, I would not have needed to beg for a few months. Finally, it was necessary to look for a quiet place to sleep.

At that moment, I felt like I had grown up and knew that I must avoid making mistakes to steer clear of trouble. My father thinks I'm really good at creating problems, so I had to be careful.

Therefore, relying on my photographic memory, I tried to memorize all the signs I encountered along the way. I counted the shops and illuminated signs. I calculated all the odd and even words. I noted the gardens and flowerbeds surrounding the station and even found a place to relieve myself. I discovered a public toilet, which I used when no one was around, disobeying, for the first time, my mother's advice, who said:

"Tobia, please, before you go out, make sure to use the bathroom because it's not nice to use other people's."

The information recorded in my mind allowed me to move independently. One day, I even reached the seafront to visit the ocean, but that vast expanse of water frightened me, and I never returned. To avoid getting lost, I tried to retrace the same path, and in the end, I found myself surrounded by a flock of pigeons pecking at crumbled cookies. Since then, feeling afraid, I have never left the station.

Not far away, I found a pizzeria where the owner discovered that I was very fond of oranges, so much so that he always gave me two. His kindness towards me proved providential, and when I went there to eat, he accepted my euro. Every now and then, he also added a glass of water, and two salad leaves for my turtles.

I even managed to find shelter for the night: I ended up in a bush of white roses, which represents loneliness in the language of flowers (another stupid statement of my teacher Dominique). However, I beheaded them one by one, which made my bed calmer.

The area was not very clean, but I didn't stop focusing on it. There was an old cardboard box that I used to cover myself, a crushed plastic bottle that I threw in the garbage can, ten cigarette butts, four filthy tissues, a piece of glass, and a dog poop.

There were many other things all around, but at some point, I felt tired. From this, I realized that my brain was no longer working; before those damn chicks arrived, I had stopped.

Under the Starry Sky

One evening, I thought I had settled comfortably in my shelter when I noticed two indistinct figures wandering suspiciously and rummaging through the bushes. They could have been two thieves, or two drug addicts, or even worse, two dangerous people who kill lonely and defenseless boys like me.

I was paralyzed with fear. I held my breath as Tommy did before blowing the famous whistle. I could feel my heart racing in my throat, echoing in my ear and then, once more, pulsing in my temples. Overcome by fear, I lost control and peed longer than I ever thought possible.

Blood flowed through the veins at 220 volts and vibrated like electric current. Just like that time I got shocked while drying my hair because a thread in the hair dryer was frayed. My mother, panicked, had time to pull the plug, saving me from certain death as a flame erupted from the device, burning my middle finger.

"Tobia, how many times do I have to tell you not to use this hair dryer? With the 220-volt shock, you crack! Do you understand that?"

"Damn shit, it almost killed you! And you, Penelope, throw away that damn hair dryer!" was my father's response, as my brothers took me away from the bathroom and calmed me down from the uproar with kisses and caresses.

"Commotion" is a word I like because my mother always uses it when she feels anxious and is unable to handle situations.

"Tobia, please, don't make all this commotion!" she says, her voice scratching in her throat.

The two men grazed my bush, wandered about, and eventually picked up some cigarette butts, which they lit. I heard them arguing, and then there was a long minute of silence.

I covered my mouth with my thumb because I felt nauseous, so I closed my eyes and moaned. The two glanced around suspiciously, and then I heard them laughing. Fortunately, a large mouse slipped between their feet to take refuge in its den.

I stayed up all night, rubbing my eyes every time they threatened to close. I'm quite skilled at this because I used to do it at home when I felt anxious in difficult situations.

Difficulties always put me in crisis because I have to make important decisions quickly, and I don't always succeed. When fear seizes me and I don't know how to act, I take off my shoes.

Once at school, I panicked because I had come across a huge dog; fortunately, Dominique grabbed me in his arms and said to me:

Calm down, Tobia; remember that you are not alone. I'm here with you. Don't be afraid. React and believe that you are stronger than everyone, even this dog!" Then he added: "Remember these rules, whenever you are in difficulty: Rule No.1 = Never let your guard down. Rule No.2 = Be ready to react. Rule No.3 = flee in case of danger. The simplest solution is always the best. Remember that!" Dominique concluded with a smile. And that evening, for the first time, I managed it on my own.

First, I did what my father repeated to me many times.

"Think, Tobia, is it possible that you can't count to ten before making a blessed decision?"

I counted to ten and decided to apply the third rule: flee in case of danger. However, those shadows moved away without noticing me. A sense of calm descended into my chest, and my heart resumed its usual rhythm.

Then, a gentleman walking by urinated behind the tree, and finally, a couple of lovers paused long enough to kiss.

I curled up in the cardboard and, before closing the lid, paused with my nose pointed up to the sky. I had never slept under the stars.

A long time ago, my teacher Giacomina had me draw the moon and many stars in my notebook; then, she had me color them yellow with finger paints. I remember that I smeared the entire page.

"But this is not a sky full of stars, Tobia!" she said, laughing out loud. "It's the sun diving into a field of ripe wheat."

So, she took my geography book and placed it in front of me. On the dark page, I saw hundreds of bright dots that formed various drawings. Then, she pointed her finger at two drawings resembling kites with hanging threads and said:

"This is Ursa Major and this is Ursa Minor!"

"Don't tell lies, bears are animals and live in the woods! You said that the other day," I replied, feeling rather annoyed.

She then told me that she was not lying; rather, since ancient times, men have created animal names for the constellations that are groupings of stars. Although these celestial bodies appear to be close to one another, they are actually very far apart. The ancients fell victim to this optical illusion and assigned names of gods, mythological heroes, and animals to those patterns.

The ancient Greeks, for example, called Ursa Major and Ursa Minor the two constellations, according to their size.

The Romans baptized Ursa Major as "Septem triones" because they saw seven oxen dragging a plough or a cart among those stars. Ursa Minor was also referred to as the wing of the Dragon, and the Greeks knew it as Cinosura, from the feminine noun Κυνόσουρα, which means "dog's tail."

Giacomina, the teacher, also told me that the most extreme star in Ursa Minor is the North Star, which coincides with the north celestial pole. That game of stargazing amused me, and Giacomina would have been proud of me because I was able to recall all those difficult names in that moment of danger!

I enjoy seeing stars. In the summer, I like searching for shooting stars in the sky. They call them the stars of San Lorenzo because they fall on the night of August tenth. I imagine that after detaching themselves from the sky, they land on Earth all in the same place. Then, I envision that where they land, they form a lake, which I named The Lake of the Stars. Teacher Giacomina told me that every star represents a desire and that if I follow my heart, my wishes will one day come true. And I have a desire: I want to be a normal guy, a guy like everyone else!

Inside my box, I found myself with my nose up, reflecting on how life is filled with desires but also troubles... and suddenly, I felt nostalgic for my Santeramo: the many walks with my family in Jazzitello, that time we picked a bunch of mushrooms in the Bosco della Parata, where I got lost... And for yet another time on the Murgia, at the Santa Lucia quarry, between Santeramo and Altamura, where the footprints of the dinosaurs were discovered...

There, too, I got into trouble by fracturing my foot. It was an accident that kept me stuck for a long time. Now, because of one of these troubles that had caused me to flee, I found myself all alone, far from home, and, moreover, in a box.

In that moment of bewilderment, I thought of my teacher, Giacomina. I considered sending her an email, like Tommy did. Except Giacomina was a real person, and I didn't have a computer with me!

With a firm gesture, I grasped the lid's edge and, while playing with the palindrome "don't nod," I finally fell asleep.

The Boy of the Oranges

– CHAPTER 22 –

In the end, I decided to take the bus home to Santeramo. I had seen several buses stop at the Bari station, with the name of my town written on the upper side of the vehicles; this made things easier.

My father claims that only those without a home sleep under bridges. I didn't sleep under bridges; instead, for fifty nights I slept under a bush of white roses and, furthermore, crouched in a cardboard box that reeked of cat urine. Every night that passed, I placed a pebble in my pocket; this way, I trained myself to count the days that had gone by and the money I had spent.

My schedule worked until I realized I had very little money. Every now and then, I took all my belongings out of my man purse to check that everything was in order. Tommy's playing cards, shoelaces, two screwdrivers, springs, some paper clips, and finally, the last euros popped up.

One day, I went to the pizzeria near the station for my usual meal and paused in front of the menu of the day. This is what I read:

"Today, September 23rd — the house offers spaghetti all'amatriciana"

That meant two things: first, that according to the date, fifty days had already passed since my escape; second, that the bar offered spaghetti. And I love spaghetti. So, during lunchtime, I showed up and ate my favorite pasta. I was very upset when the waiter asked me for five euros for the meal.

This meant that I would have been left with just over five euros. It was an odd sum, and this was not good.

The man, with reddish and shriveled skin, looked at me and said: "What's up? Didn't you like them?"

"I like spaghetti," I replied, looking down, as I can't stand it when people look me straight in the eye.

Then, I added:

"I thought that today *the house offered spaghetti*. So it is written."

"Oh, boy, you've got a good nerve!" replied the man in surprise. Then, with a still and dry face, he looked at me with his little black and lively eyes and added:

"Well, but we know each other. It has been a long time since we last saw you. I recognize you, you know; you're the boy of the oranges, aren't you?"

"I like oranges. You have always been so kind to offer me Coke and water as well. I don't have a lot of money, so I save money," I replied, looking out the window.

"Do you live around here?" he asked abruptly, while he wiped the counter of coffee stains.

My heart stopped for a moment as I formulated incoherent sentences amid the meticulously set tables. Seizing a moment when I felt unobserved, I downed a glass of wine. He stood on a table adorned with baskets full of freesias, anemones, and lavender.

The flowers glistened under the neon light, and I regarded them with suspicion. I could already hear Dominique's voice explaining their meanings: freesias for friendship, anemones for desolation, and lavender for trust..., but I continued to see in them only Mrs. Cristina!

"Do you live around here?" the man resumed, raising the tone of his voice and bringing me back to reality.

"Not really," I replied.

Then, I saw that he picked up the phone and dialed a number. Finally, he said to me:

"Okay, for this time the house offers you spaghetti, but understand that offering doesn't always mean that things are free. In a restaurant, it means that it is the dish of the day." Then, as he usually did, he took two large oranges and offered them to me:

"Here are the usual oranges, too. For today, everything is free."

"Thank you, sir. You are very kind."

But he insisted:

"Why are you in such a bad shape?"

"Like what, sir?" I said, but I knew full well that he was referring to my muddy shoes and tousled hair.

"You're so dirty... You should wash more!" And, after a pause, he continued, "Do you know that you look a lot like the photo of a boy I saw this morning posted on the wall of the station? The whole city is full of them. Did you run away from home, by any chance!?"

Mom says that when people ask too many questions, it means they are becoming curious, which may not be good. I felt my brain go haywire, so I started counting to figure out how to respond. However, after I reached ten, I still didn't have an answer ready, even though my instinct told me not to let my guard down.

"Do you have any salad leaves for Brilly and Loly?" I asked, instead.

"And who am I?" said the man, stopping talking on the phone.

"But my turtles!" I replied, disappointed, as I took the two turtles out of the box. While doing this, I counted three cups of coffee, three teaspoons, three sachets of sugar, a rose that had faded in the plastic jar, and three customers talking in a low voice.

One of the three customers, with a thin and stiff body, paid and said:

"Keep the rest." Then, turning to me, "Will you let me through, please?"

I paused for a moment to figure out where to place my feet to make some room, and at the same time, I heard the other customer saying:

"But this kid looks like the picture on the poster!"

"Yes, it looks like him!" replied the third.

Three is an odd number, so I thought I might be in trouble.

I placed the tin box with Brilly and Loly in my pocket, took the two oranges, and walked toward the exit. When I turned around, I found myself facing two men coming directly toward me.

"It's him, the boy of the oranges..." said the man behind the counter with a smile.

"Yes, it's him!" confirmed one of the customers.

It was then that I began to swing and count mentally, and at four, I fled. I crossed the room, moving past the tables, but the third customer tripped me, causing me to stumble and fall.

The two gentlemen approached me and lifted me up. Then, in a gentle tone, they said:

"Did you hurt yourself, boy?"

I yanked them because they had taken me by the shoulders, and I can't stand being touched, especially by strangers.

"I didn't do anything. I didn't steal Mrs. Cristina's ring," I said.

"What's this ring story?!" they both replied, looking at each other.

"Mrs. Cristina's," I whimpered, as my thoughts mingled with the peeping of the usual chicks. Before realizing they were two strange policemen, I picked up the two oranges that had rolled on the ground and threw them against the window, which shattered into a thousand pieces.

To Police Commissioner Lolita Lobosco, then Finally Home!

At the Bari Police Headquarters, the picture blow-up was attached to the wall, and in that portrait, it appeared that I was present. Beneath it, something like this was written: Tobia comes home – we love you.

I crouched on the first chair I found, directly in front of the poster. There was no doubt about it; it was my photo from the day of my First Communion. I had a smiling face and a well-groomed appearance. My clean, regular face was framed by short, golden hair that barely covered my ears; my mouth, with its fleshy, pronounced lips, hinted at a smile. Finally, my cross-eyed eyes were hidden behind a blue-framed pair of glasses that rested on a long, crooked nose.

I remember that my mother, at the shot, had told me:

"Tobia, laugh a little. You have such a long nose!"

I hinted at a slight smile, so much so that my lips took on a slightly crooked appearance, revealing my upper incisors. On the wall, there were also various posters that I cannot describe now.

Then, I heard a door opening and a woman's voice saying:

"So, Tony, have you found him?"

"Of course, Chief, he is here! Esposito and I picked it up at the station, in the pizzeria. It's him, the boy on the poster. The brat who escaped from *the "Garden of Happy Boys,"* and whose traces had been lost..."

"God bless him, the nightmare is over! The parents are coming. They are so worried, poor things."

It was then that I saw her: long raven hair, vivid eyes, and a bra like Giacomina's. On her feet, she wore heels so high that, as my mother says, she seemed to live on the twelfth floor. I couldn't believe it. It was her, Police Commissioner Lolita Lobosco. At that moment, I thought that perhaps beneath it all was the hand of that big baby, my father.

For my escape, he managed to get the interest of even the commissioner he liked so much.

"So, are you Tobia Barbato?" she attacked, without much ado.

"Uhmmm..."

"The young man who ran away from the Institute...?"

"Uhmmm..."

"Young man..."

I thought I could hear my mother.

"Darn it, answer."

While she pressed me with questions, intent on sticking her nose in my affairs, I walked over to her desk and paused to admire a beautiful basket full of oranges.

"Don't tell me. Do you like oranges?"

At my assent, she nodded her head and handed one to me.

"Two, please," I said, adjusting my man purse over my shoulder.

"Well done to Tobia. Dear young man, we have discovered that you know how to speak. Tell me why you ran away from the Institute?"

Noticing my silence, which was rather obstinate, she added:

"Come on, tell Lolita about you."

I counted and recounted the letters that formed her name, Lo-li-ta, excluding the surname, and they were even. Then I concluded that I might as well tell her the whole truth since she had decided not to give up. I wanted to make it clear that I was completely innocent and that being a kleptomaniac did not necessarily mean being a thief. On the contrary, it was my intention to find the real culprit behind the theft. So, while I peeled the orange and ate the wedges two by two, I told her everything.

"Jesus, let me tell you, what a bad trouble you have gotten into. It is not possible that my Carabinieri colleagues have made this mistake! How did they do it, I just don't know. Listen, your case is under the jurisdiction of the Carabinieri of Santeramo, but I want to help you. I will talk to them, and we will decide what to do. You are going home, for now. Do you hear me?" And so saying, she too slipped a few orange wedges into her mouth.

"Two," she specified. "Because I like even numbers too!" Then she added:

"Tony, what's all this racket?"

They were my parents.

"Here you are at last, Tobia! God be thanked. I thought I would never see you again! Oh, Tobia. Tobia."

It was my mother's voice that, upon seeing me, took my face in her hands and burst into great tears.

My father, who usually never shows weakness, ruffled my hair and said:

"A misfortune could have happened... Anyway, we have to thank the commissioner. We owe it to her if you are here now." Then, looking at me more closely, he added: "Where the hell have you been? You look like a piglet that has rolled in the mud. Right at home, a nice shower with a super grooming. For now, however, let's go and settle the bill with the owner of the pizzeria, where you broke the window!"

Then he blew his nose so hard that he resembled a trumpeter; he expressed his emotion this way when he didn't get the usual stomach acid. Even my brothers stuck by me and vowed that they would never let me go again. I, however, wanted to clarify my position regardless.

"I'm never going back to the Center..."

"Okay, okay. Quiet... We also clarified this with Dr. Lobosco. We have informed Mr. Martino that we have located you. We told him we have no intention of bringing you back there."

Then he turned to the Commissioner and, raising his voice, added: "Is it true, Commissioner, that Tobia is never coming back to the Institute?"

"Of course, it's true. But, Tobia, can you come to your Lolita from time to time?!"

And smiling, she took two more oranges from the basket and handed them to me. "What can I do, my handsome? I have a tender heart. And please, when you eat them, think of me!" Before letting me go, she planted two kisses on my cheeks.

"But now let's go home!" my father intervened, insisting that I get into the car.

I was so tired that I fell asleep as soon as the car moved. When Mom shook me, I heard her voice saying:

"Wake up, Tobia. We have arrived".

I dragged myself to the entrance with difficulty. Then, as soon as I stepped into the living room, I suddenly woke up. I felt betrayed; all the furniture had been rearranged.

The sideboard was replaced by the two-seater sofa, where I usually lie down when I feel like thinking. The table was centered in the room instead of its usual corner, and the same applied to the living room as well.

"Where's the cupboard?" I said with some anxiety in my voice.

"Ugh, I knew it, here we go again!" replied my father, closing the door.

"The cupboard is in the kitchen, Tobia. Please don't create problems for yourself. You are still at home. Come on, don't worry!" replied the mother, conciliatory.

"We changed the position of the furniture to create more space. It's the same thing, really!" my father added.

And no, that was not the same thing.

I felt upset, so I began yelling and pounding on the door for help, just like when I have to put on my underwear by myself and can't.

In my house, there is only one rule: everything must remain as I have learned to see since birth. The furnishings must stay in their designated places, and woe to any changes.

When Mom does the heavy cleaning, I'm always there to ensure that everything is put back in the right place. I almost always arrange the objects in the house as I prefer. However, my family's needs do not always coincide with mine.

I thought my room had also changed. I rushed inside; at least that part remained as it was. I took the box with Brilly and Loly out of my man purse and slipped it under the bed. Then, I urged my parents to return the furniture to its original place, and by the time everything was back in order, dawn had already arrived. Finally, I found the bunches of wisteria that my mother had placed in the ceramic vase to welcome me quite pleasing, and I lay down on the bed where I soon fell asleep.

I dreamed of Tommy not wanting to be disturbed because he was struggling with his solitaire. Then I dreamed of Madame Fantasy messing up all his cards. Tommy got angry and threw the two of cups at her. Then, Mr. Martino came and said:

"**Tobia**, why did you flee? **Tobia**, you are guilty now. **Tobia** returns... **Tobia!**"

I woke up, startled. It was my mother trying to wake me.

"Tobia, wake up! Come, the shower is waiting for you. You smell like a goat..."

"Don't touch me," I said, annoyed, "I'll do it myself!"

I sat on the edge of the bed and took off my pajamas. Then I didn't scream, didn't protest, and, naked as a worm, I slipped under the boiling water, anticipating a plate of spaghetti with sauce, sausage, and the two juicy oranges that my Lolita had given me.

Back to School

– CHAPTER 24 –

When I returned to school, I planned to devise a strategy to uncover the true perpetrator of the theft. I found this approach enjoyable. For a while, everything went smoothly.

At school, I ran into Dominique, who was happy to see me again. Most importantly, I met my friend Pilù, who, seeing me with my friend Maria, said:

"Here's Maria, that stupid cow."

"Pier Luca, keep your tongue at bay!" said Dominique, clapping him on the shoulder.

Maria wore jeans with the word "love" on her ass and had the usual air of a nice girl. When she saw me, she approached with a smile on her face, but I stepped back to keep her from touching me, even though my heart raced at the sight of her. Then, Michael arrived and was so stiff toward me that it seemed like he had swallowed a broomstick.

My class turned out to be louder than usual. Everyone wanted to know about my escape and the adventures I had experienced. However, the noise, the shouting, and the general clamoring clashed too much with my auditory perception, so Dominique took me to our classroom, the one marked with the symbol H.

There, just as I had left them, I found all my belongings in order. The only novelty was the presence of a huge sign on the ceramic vase full of flowers with the words "Say it with a flower!"

Seeing my hesitation, Dominique invited me in. Then he said:

"You know, Tobia, flowers have a language that can be useful when we can't find the right words to express ourselves."

"I don't like flowers!" I replied dryly. "They all have Mrs. Cristina's face!"

He disregarded my sentence.

"So, what do we do?" said Dominique, opening the notebook.

"I want to find out who stole the ring," I said.

"The ring?" he replied.

"Mrs. Cristina's solitaire ring."

"Ah, that's it. Is that why you fled the center?" he asked.

It was one of those questions that already contained the answer. Meanwhile, he set the notebook on the desk.

Inside, I recognized my handwriting, which unfolded in a child-like manner, with letters in block form. I used to fill in the white staves haphazardly, facing the sheet directly with my impressions. On one page, my themes were there:

Theme n.1

Tobia does not want to get up in the morning. His mother goes to his room and wakes him up. Tobia turns away; He says it's cold and he's still sleepy.

Theme n.2

Tobia and his father fly high in the blue sky.

Theme n.3

Sweet mother, you hold a special place in Tobia's heart. When you're not around, how much he wishes you were! He offers you this golden star to show that you are his most precious treasure and to express how deeply he loves you. With everlasting affection, Tobia.

It was followed by a star-shaped design.

Dominique had pinned a note underneath: **you were good, but rewrite everything in the first person...**

Another page listed the countries with their capitals. For example: **Ireland** ---- Dublin; **Romania** ---- Bucharest; **United Kingdom** ---- London; **Ukraine** ---- Kyiv, and so on.

On yet another page, there were all the brands of cars I knew, and, in this, I am unbeatable: Fiat 500; Fiat Uno; Fiat Punto; Fiat Brava. Renault Twingo; Seat Ibiza; Seat Marbella; Rover; Toyota.

Then there was a recipe invented by me that I never completed.
Tuna appetizer :
500 grams of fresh tuna
Lemon
(2) bay leaves
A handful of parsley
A grated carrot
Half a cup of oil
A clove of garlic
A handful of capers
Eight slices of bread
    — *P.S. Salt just enough*

Dominique says that *P.S.* stands for Post Scriptum, a Latin word, which means written after. It is used at the end of a letter or communication to add or clarify something that has been forgotten.

Then there was the even number line. There were no odd numbers, but they were replaced by a question mark. Thus:

0___?___2____?___4___?___6___?___8___?___10

Finally, there was a little problem that I had solved brilliantly because the sum was naturally equal:

Problem: *In front of our school are several trees: three are tall and three are short. How many trees are there in total?*

Solution: *In front of our school, there are a total of six trees.*

Then Dominique added, "Very well, very well. Now, turn the page, Tobia, let's plan the investigation. If you want to find out who stole Mrs. Cristina's ring, you need to get organized!"

And, reminding me of my mother's tedious lessons on Edgar Allan Poe's detective story, where the narrator specifies that "The important thing is to know what to observe" because the action "does not lie in the validity of the deduction, but in the quality of the observation"—with the meticulousness of a policeman, I wrote:

Action number one: *Return to the scene of the theft*
Action number two: *Talk to Mrs. Cristina*
Action number three: *Draw conclusions*

"Bravo, Tobia. You have character and backbone!"

I didn't understand what Dominique meant, but I liked that definition. Before closing the notebook, in action one, I counted: twenty-two vowels and twenty consonants. In action two: twenty vowels and twenty-two consonants. In action three: sixteen vowels and eighteen consonants. They were all even numbers, and I felt very satisfied.

Then, I reached out and, quick as lightning, tossed all of Dominique's flowers out of the window.

Archimedes' Principle

I put on my shirt, adjusted my underwear, and slipped into my pants. Then, I donned my socks and pulled them up as high as I could above the knee. The heel, as usual, sat on the instep, but I chose to ignore it. I always dress this way. I laced up my shoes and headed to the kitchen: like every morning, breakfast was already set on the table.

"But what are you doing? Look at how you put on your socks!" grumbled my mother as I sat down at the table. I didn't listen to her. As always, I dipped the cookie into the milk, and the liquid jumped up before spreading across the table. It was a game I invented a few days ago. I wanted to find out why the milk skipped when the biscuit arrived.

Dominique had explained to me and re-explained that the biscuit obeyed the rules of physics, specifically Archimedes' principle: a body immersed in a liquid experiences an upward vertical thrust equal in intensity to the weight of the displaced fluid volume. In other words, the biscuit displaces the milk and floats or sinks depending on whether its specific gravity is lower or greater than that of the liquid in which it is immersed. By the same principle, a ship floats rather than sinks. Conversely, if the specific weight of the body is greater than that of the liquid, the latter sinks, as happens with a stone thrown into a pond.

The concept was clear. Almost.

Then I wondered what would happen to Mrs. Cristina's ring if it ended up in a glass of water. It would certainly sink. And like a frame, my mind began to remember...

That morning, I arrived at Mrs. Cristina's building ahead of my friends. One after another, they arrived: Pilù, Michael, and Xavier.

We were standing by the front door, and with the parrot, as often happened, we made a great noise. I looked out into the hallway, and I saw something shining on the counter where Mrs. Cristina usually worked. I recognized her ring, which shimmered in the sunlight that filtered through the window. Then, one of my friends asked Mrs. Cristina for a glass of water.

Although she was angry because we teased her parrot, she entered the room next to his cage and filled a disposable glass with water. She adjusted the headset that hung three-quarters of the way down, and as she answered the phone with her lips dangling, she said:

"Hey, you, the glass is on top of the counter. If you want to drink, take it. Then throw it in the recycling bin!"

Then, there was a noise, and when I looked back into the cage to see what had happened, the ring was gone. In its place, there was a large spill of water.

My friends Michael and Xavier left while Pilù and I stayed behind with the struggling parrot.

Chicorita had caught her neck in the bars of her cage and was thrashing desperately. She would have suffocated if I had not freed her.

It was then that Mrs. Cristina arrived, screaming and demanding her ring. Pilù fled with his legs up, while I remained her prisoner. And, as people flocked in, drawn back by her screams, she accused me of the theft.

I dipped another biscuit into the milk and sank it, spilling the milk again. Now I understood how things had really gone: whoever had stolen the ring had used the glass of water, dipping the jewel into it. The potential thieves of the ring were the only people present: Michael, Xavier, and, alas, Pilù.

When I told Dominique about my discovery, he praised me. However, he also pointed out that if I intended to accuse someone, I needed to gather evidence.

"You know, Tobia, the ring was unfortunately found in your man purse. Now you have to prove who stole the ring and why they put it there. But above all, why did he do it?"

In short, as mom says, it was a tough nut to crack! Then I thought that I was a kleptomaniac and, therefore, it was hardly credible that I was innocent. This made everything more difficult.

I remembered Tommy's words, so I said:

"Maybe whoever put it in my bag was on the verge of being discovered and took advantage of the chance he had. So, he felt in danger and thought of hiding it in a safe place, which in this case was my man purse, getting me into trouble."

"That may be," Dominique replied. "Maybe."

The next day was Sunday, and as usual, I attended Mass with my parents. After the service, the priest gave the blessing, and Mom, Dad, and I focused on making the sign of the cross. While I searched for the words to say in the name of the Father, the Son, and the Holy Spirit, I felt very nervous because I remembered that I had to return to Mrs. Cristina's building to investigate and organize all the papers, as my father mentioned.

My Investigation

– CHAPTER 26 –

Several days passed before I could start my investigation. One morning, on my way to school, I stopped near Mrs. Cristina's building. The parrot was gone, and the door was shut. I walked around the block twice, then paused. Everything was quiet. I looked at the street, the building, the entrance; everything had remained unchanged except for the clear absence of Chicorita.

Since the theft occurred, Mrs. Cristina no longer put her parrot outside, preventing the boys from stopping there as they had in the past.

A neighbor, Mrs. Sara, an old yellowish spinster with a fat ass and small tits, famous throughout the neighborhood for her gossip and avarice, seeing me, said:

"What are you doing here? Shouldn't you be at school?"

"I was looking for Chicorita, but she's not there".

"How do you not know?" she said. "That poor little animal was continually tyrannized. And then, boys who entered, boys who came out of the door of the building... It was an indecency. Poor Mrs. Cristina!"

"Oh, too bad!" I said, "It was fun to play with Chicorita."

"Yes, but not everyone behaved like good guys. Some were exaggerating." Then, looking at her mismatched slippers and her blouse buttoned sideways, just as I do when I'm not very careful with my dressing, she added: "Do you want to come in?"

I remembered that my mother had forbidden me from having conversations with people I knew little about.

"Tobia, it doesn't feel good sneaking into other people's houses," she would say whenever she noticed the urge to explore unfamiliar environments in my eyes.

"Thank you, Mrs. Sara, but my mother says that it is not good to enter someone else's house. And then, I must inspect the place of the theft," I said.

As I told her this, I mentally counted the letters that formed her name. They were even: two vowels and two consonants, so Mrs. Sara deserved all my trust. I knew that slightly funny lady, having seen her every morning behind the glass of her window. So much so that in the end, when I looked in her direction, she always greeted me by waving her hand, her head framed by something strange that I recognized as curlers.

"Oh, Tobia, but we know each other!" she said. "You are the boy of the oranges. You always have an orange in your hand when you play with the parrot."

"Two," I corrected her. "I like even numbers."

But she ignored my answer and added:

"The theft? Ah, yes. I have heard of it. Oh, if you want, I could help you. From here, I always see everything. I don't miss anything, you know? Nowadays, we are no longer at peace. It's a terrible, really terrible thing to take advantage of a single lady," she said, adjusting her blouse. Then she took a white handkerchief fresh from the laundry out of her bra and blew her nose, which was dripping like the faucet in my house.

"Sorry, I have a cold," she justified herself, slipping a candy into her mouth.

That gesture reminded me of my father, who, when excited, always blows his nose and takes a Maalox tablet for his stomach acid.

Mrs. Sara, quite advanced in age, lived on the ground floor. The front door opened directly into the living room, where she spent entire days observing everything that happened outside her home by simply pulling back the curtain. From the window, she watched her neighbors performing their chores: the doorkeeper, like Mrs. Cristina, the urchins who chased her, calling her "Old hag," and the street sweepers who cleaned the streets.

In this way, she was aware of all the facts and misdeeds in the neighborhood. My father called her a gossip and a rather refined ruffian, so she needed to be kept a mile away from our house. In short, she was someone who meddled in other people's affairs.

At the time, I thought this could be useful for the investigation because she would be what is called an eyewitness. My father says that gossipy and pimping people could turn out to be a double-edged sword: if you are a nice person, they defend you; if, on the other hand, you turn out to be an unpleasant person, they accuse you.

"And what do you have to do with the story of the theft, Tobia?" she continued, arching her eyebrows.

"I'm sorry, but I can't tell you." Then I paused for a moment, and fearing that she might think I was actually the thief of the ring, I added, "But your name corresponds to an even number, so I'm confident you're fine, and I'll tell you."

She looked at me, puzzled, then said:

What is this story about my name corresponding to an even number?

"Well," I said, "it's simple. It is made up of two consonants and two vowels, so the sum is always even."

"Do you know you're a weird guy? Oh, you wouldn't be the guy they accused of... Yes, in short... do you understand!?"

Not having the courage to answer, I nodded.

"Oh, poor baby. How could they do such a thing to you! Because it wasn't you; am I right?" she said, sure she received a nod of assent from me.

"Poor dear, do you want to tell me about it?"

Maybe I shouldn't have done it, but I told Mrs. Sara, in detail, all my misadventures. Then she put her hand to her mouth and said:

"Oh, my dear, I'm so sorry! You didn't deserve any of this." Pausing on those words, she added: "I recall that day."

"You mean that you saw everything?" I said, heartened that she liked me.

"Yes, I was here behind this window, and I can swear I saw you free Chicorita's neck from the bars of the cage. I remember you stuffed oranges in your pocket to free your hands. I also remember your friends escaping. I'm sorry, Tobia; I should have told Mrs. Cristina. I really think I should have."

Mrs. Sara pulled the handkerchief from her bra again and blew her nose vigorously once more.

She was the kindest gossip and ruffian I'd ever known!

Over Mrs. Cristina

They say I am a difficult boy, suffering from a sharp decline in social integration and communication. The barrier that separates me from others is called *Autism*, but it doesn't need to be acknowledged. My special needs professor informed me that, recently, scientists have replaced this term with the label ASD, which is not the name of a dishwashing detergent but refers to "Autism Spectrum Disorders." This is merely to indicate a condition whose causes are hard to identify.

Professor Dominique, however, states that there is nothing wrong with this because scientists such as Einstein, Newton, and Steve Jobs—just to name a few—were autistic and faced their challenges with constant commitment. He also mentions that I can do it very well because I am a boy with a decisive character, fussy, and intelligent, even if I can be stubborn like an old mule. In short, I may be a bit repetitive, but I am very intelligent. "You are a star on earth!" he always repeats when I'm nervous. He also says that if I give it my all, I can become a good investigator, and this could be my future job.

I told him that I liked his opinion, but that not everyone thought like him.

However, knowing that things always follow a precise order gives me confidence and helps me overcome anxiety. Clarity also makes me more decisive because I understand what I should or shouldn't do. For this reason, I decided to uncover the perpetrator of the theft because I couldn't tolerate this significant lie about me. My dignity was at risk of being compromised forever, and as someone who values precision, I could not accept it.

Solving the problem had become a matter of life and death. My father often tells me:

"Tobia, it's better to live a day as a lion than a hundred as a sheep!"

So I decided to live my day like a lion, going to my accuser's house; it was a risk I had to take. I determined that Detective Tobia needed to uncover the culprit.

Mrs. Cristina always wore a pair of tattered trousers that were very comfortable for the work she did. When she opened the door, she had a cap on her head resembling a rooster's comb that kept her hair back. She was sweeping the staircase leading to the upper floors when I arrived. She leaned the broom against the wall, and, adjusting her glasses, she showed me her hand with the ring that had been returned to her after the discovery in my man purse.

"Damn it!" she uttered, placing both hands on his hips, just like my mother does, when she investigates my brothers' misdeeds. Visibly surprised, she added, "What are you doing here?"

I heard the radio playing a concert by David Garrett from one of his albums: Encore. He's a musician who excites me because David plays the violin in a crazy way. He is a genius for combining classical music with rock.

"Mrs. Cristina, I'm sorry, but I came to tell you that it wasn't me who stole your ring," I said, listening to the radio.

She looked me over from head to toe as if I were a Martian. Then, she began scratching everywhere: first on her nose, then on her ear, and finally on her belly, making each gesture seem ridiculous. At last, she straightened her crest, which, as usual, hung three-quarters of the way down, and speaking slowly, she said:

"Come in, what are you doing there, stiff like a baccalà!"

"I don't usually go into strangers' homes," I replied.

"But you like music!" she said in a persuasive voice.

"I like David Garrett!" I replied.

"Ah, is that his name?"

"Yes, his music is exceptional. He plays the violin in a unique way, and I love his concerts."

"So... You want me to believe that it wasn't you who stole my ring?" she said, changing the subject. Then she looked at her hand with the jewel and added: "So it wasn't you who stole it!"

"No, ma'am, it wasn't me, and I'm here to carry out an investigation."

"Ah!" was her answer.

"I would like to reconstruct that morning with you."

"Ah!" she answered again.

I knew she was looking at me with some skepticism and waiting for me to leave of my own accord. But I added: "The carabinieri have made a mistake."

"Oh, my God!" she answered.

"I'm sure it was one of my friends who was here with me, who stole your ring. But I swear I didn't know anything at all!"

"Oh, my God!" replied Mrs. Cristina again.

"And I was also able to figure out how he stole it from you!" I continued.

"Really?" she said, as the conversation became interesting.

"Yes. One of my friends asked you for a glass of water."

"Really?" she replied again, sitting down on the chair in the watch box.

"And when you answered the phone, one of my friends took the ring, which you had carelessly left on the bench, and dropped it into the water, appropriating it."

"Oh Lord God!" she stammered in amazement.

"According to Archimedes' principle, the ring, being heavier than the amount of water, settled on the bottom and the displaced water poured onto the counter," I explained to her, specifically.

"According to whose principle?" she said, still stunned.

"Archimedes!" I replied.

"Oh, Archimedes," she pretended to know.

"At least now you know it wasn't me," I concluded with that explanation, feeling satisfied.

"You're Tobia, aren't you? The boy with oranges..." she said, recovering.

"Yes. I'm Tobia Barbato, and I live across the block. My parents took me to a rehabilitation center so that I could fill out those boring psychological tests and regain my serenity with the help of experienced people..." I said.

"Oh, I'm sorry!" she resumed.

"Because of your ring," I added.

"Oh, I'm sorry!" she repeated.

"But I ran away. You know, to clarify," I said.

"Oh, Tobia, I'm sorry," she concluded. Then, she got up and opened a drawer. She took a button with a thread hanging on it and handed it to me.

"Hold this, " she said, "perhaps it may be useful for your investigations. I found it on the floor, near the counter, that day. Surely it belongs to the real thief of my ring. I'm sorry, but I always forgot to hand it over to the carabinieri."

"Well, the interrogation is over," I said, "now I have to go."

"Tobia!" she called, as I walked away.

"Yes, Mrs. Cristina?"

"You're a smart guy. I wanted to tell you!" and, politely, she took two oranges from the basket of the watch box and handed them to me.

"Thank you," I replied, "my support teacher, Dominique, who is helping me in the investigation, also tells me so." Saying this, I took the oranges and left.

Before leaving, I stopped to look at the flowers I had destroyed, and I was stunned: they had wonderfully recovered!

The Button,
The Body of Evidence

– CHAPTER 28 –

The doors of my house have no keys. I take and keep them in my man purse, including the one from the piano that my mother bought for my brother Matthew, which has been lying there for centuries without anyone bothering to play it.

The other day, Mom went to the bathroom and, as usual, grumbled:

"Tobia, give me the key."

After a while, she continued:

"I wonder… what do you do with all the keys you take away from the doors!?"

Her statement was not a question, but rather a reflection expressed aloud. Adults often resort to reflections expressed aloud, especially when they prefer not to address the topic at hand directly.

But the answer is simple: there are those who collect coins, those who collect antique furniture, and those who collect stamps, like my school friend Michael (he has many albums in which he arranges them in order of date and value). I collect keys.

Mom isn't the only one snooping into my things; now my professor Dominique is involved too. Just the other day, in my support room, I emptied my bag's contents onto the table and sorted through my toys. I placed all the expired phone cards to the right of the table and all the keys on the left. In the center, I put both the green and red screwdrivers. I also grouped the two pens I had taken from my father, the six dice from my brother's board games, and the various scattered objects I collected while my mother was distracted: two ceramic kittens, a toothpick, and many pieces of paper. Finally, I spotted a medium-sized brown button with thread hanging from it; it was the button that Mrs. Cristina had given me to continue the investigation. In the middle were four holes where the cotton had been sewn several times, and this was a good clue because the holes were even.

Dominique looked at the whole thing and said:

"Tobia, do you also collect buttons now?"

"This is the proof of my innocence!" I said. Then, I took the button for the thread and swung it like a pendulum.

I let the button continue to swing before my eyes, forming a wide and imaginary semicircle. It was a gesture I often made when I concentrated: I needed it to build a thought with a logical thread.

I noticed that under the buttonhole, there was some frayed fabric, also brown. This indicated that the jacket had to be the same color.

So, I took my notebook and, among *the conclusions* I had outlined with Dominique, I wrote: *"Brown buton with four holes, with hanging thread and brown fabric under the holes"*.

"You're a smart guy, Tobia. However, add another *t* to the word *button*," he said, with a note of pride in his voice.

Dominique, meanwhile, had replaced the teacher Giacomina for quite a while. By then, I had grown up and was attending high school, where Dominique followed me. In fact, he was a really nice guy with a fascination with flowers and smelled like lavender.

The teacher Giacomina, on the other hand, was no longer a substitute teacher and taught at an elementary school in a town near mine. When she left, I was so sorry that I started throwing tantrums again whenever I had to do my homework.

One day, my father lost his temper and shook me with these words:

"Tobia, do you want to understand that life changes? One day, you get up and realize that nothing is the same anymore. Is it possible that everything is so difficult for you? Get over it, darn it!"

I looked again at the button dangling from my hand. Then I thought it was very similar to the one I had seen hanging from Pilù's jacket. Finally, I considered Mrs. Sara, who would testify in my favor. I believed that, at last, I would be free from that unbearable accusation of being considered a thief. In the end, I remembered that I also needed to write an email to the teacher Giacomina to let her know.

I began to feel better now that my investigation was progressing well. I had to follow the pattern I had built in my head, step by step. Therefore, it was necessary to wait for my friend Pilù to return from Rome, where he had gone to visit his father, who was in the hospital. Only then would I understand whether he was the real thief of the ring. In the meantime, I suffered at the mere thought that my best friend had betrayed me.

I felt like the time I tumbled down the stairs and scraped my knees, with my mother having to apply a bottle of ice to stop the hematoma. Meanwhile, I felt my head throb with tremendous pain.

But as my father had told me about the teacher Giacomina, I had to get over it for my friend Pilù as well. To be honest, however, I didn't really understand what "get over it" meant.

In the hours when I was alone, reflecting on what to do, I listened to the rhythm of my breathing, counted the beats of my heart, and inhaled the scent of my skin. Then, I put the first orange wedge in my mouth, followed by another and another... They all rolled down my tongue, unchewed, ending up in my stomach. I swallowed vigorously, wedge after wedge, and, after the tenth, I vomited them all onto the floor.

It was an absolute miracle I didn't die!

The Odds of
Extended Families

Pilù returned to school when I had lost all hope of checking whether his jacket was truly missing a button. I learned from Dominique that his father had passed away, which saddened me because Pilù's family was struggling financially.

Perhaps this is why Pilù did not have a good reputation; he had a habit of stealing something wherever he went. Therefore, when I asked my father to bring my friend home, he often responded:

"Tobia, don't take it badly, I don't want that boy in the house because where he has eyes, he has hands!"

Only later did I understand that it was a way of saying to emphasize that he stole. This strengthened my suspicion that, without a doubt, he was the thief of the ring. However, I needed proof because, as my support teacher Dominique had taught me, you can't accuse anyone without evidence. I had been unlucky because the carabinieri had found the jewel in my man purse, and this was certain proof.

Now Pilù was in even more trouble, with his father dead, a stepmother who was about to remarry, and no one who cared for him anymore. I felt somewhat sorry for his situation. After all, he was the same age as I and lived abandoned; yet I couldn't forgive him for getting me into trouble, which led to my unjust accusation of a theft I didn't commit.

"You see, Tobia," Dominique said one day, "your friend should be helped. His life is not easy, now that he is an orphan, and his step-mother does not worry much about his future."

"What do you mean orphan?" I said, jotting down the word in my Italian notebook.

"When someone loses one or both parents!" he stated.

"But Pilù has a mom!" I replied.

"That's true, but it's not his mother who gave birth to him!" he insisted. Then, Dominique explained to me what had happened to my friend. Pier Luca lost his mother shortly after he was born, and his father remarried; that's why he had another mother, whom he called stepmother. However, his father was no longer there either. But I already knew all of this.

"Ok," I said, "But my friend Michael told me that he has two mothers."

"For Michael, it's different," he interjected. "His parents are separated, and he lives with his real dad and a new mom. Those, Tobia, are called extended families!"

I was starting to have difficulty understanding his explanations. Then Dominique scratched his head and, taking my face in his hands, said:

"You see, Tobia, it's like calculating probabilities... It is not a simple matter, but I will try to explain to you:

First Probability: it is that two parents, after marriage, always remain together, and in this case, the children who are born have the same father and the same mother.

Second Probability: one parent may die, and the other may remarry. In this case, as happened to your friend Pier Luigi, the new parent replaces the one who is no longer there.

Third Probability: that two parents, no longer getting along with each other, separate. In this circumstance, both can remain alone or remarry and thus form new families, just like what happened to your friend Michael. That's why he has two mothers.

Fourth Probability: two married individuals, even if they have children of their own by choice, can decide to become adoptive parents."

It seemed like a very complicated story. However, adults always manage their lives in complicated ways. For instance, what did adoptive parents mean? Since it was a term I had often heard from my parents, I asked Dominique without thinking too much about it.

He scratched his head once more and, taking a deep breath, said:

"Ah, I see that today you are particularly curious! However, adoptive parents are those who choose to raise children who are alone in the world."

At that moment, Pilù arrived. He held a sandwich in his hand and bit into it as if he hadn't eaten in a long time, while in the other hand, he carried a bunch of mimosa, which he placed on the counter.

"Ciao!" he said.

I didn't answer. Although I was sorry for what had happened to him, I was a little angry with my friend.

"I'm glad to see you. How are you?" he continued, offering me some of his sandwich and bringing the mimosa closer to me.

I shook my head because I never take anything from others, and I never eat food that is not mine.

"I'm sorry, Tobia. I regret what you went through. I just found out that you've been in that dreadful institute and managed to escape," he added, not pausing for my response.

I started to feel nervous because Pilù did not have his jacket, and I couldn't compare the button that Mrs. Cristina had given me with hers. I didn't want to say anything that might offend him, so I stayed quiet, but I glanced sideways at the patch of golden light resting on the desk.

As usual, Dominique intervened:

"Thank you, Pier Luca, for the mimosa. You're a really sensitive guy. A nice gesture to your friend Tobia, whom we all believe to be innocent!"

And with those words, he had once again had his say.

A Basketball Game

– CHAPTER 30 –

Michael, a boy with a large head but low intelligence, called me "handicapped" the other day. At that word, I lost my composure and shouted at him:

"Shut up, you ugly bastard!" Then, before I could keep the annoying buzzing in my head at bay, I jumped on him and thrashed the living daylight out of him. It happened during Physical Education class, while we were playing basketball.

Dominique ruled that it was foolish to call a person "handicapped" and to beat someone. He was not wrong; however, in life, you also must defend yourself, especially to avoid becoming a victim of injustice. And I hate injustice.

Basketball is played by two teams of five players each. Our team includes Pilù, Michael, Xavier, Maria, and me. In contrast, the opposing team consists of five boys from different classes. Each team must score in the opponent's basket while preventing the rival team from gaining possession of the ball. The main purpose of the game is to score points.

The ball can be passed, shot, served, rolled, or dribbled in any direction. However, everything must be done in compliance with the regulations. If the ball touches any person or goes outside the boundary line, it is considered out of bounds.

It happened that during a decisive moment of the game, I took possession of the ball, and after a short dribble, I threw it into the basket *of the enemy*, as we used to say between ourselves. But the ball swirled several times around the edge of the basket and finally, instead of going in, it bounced out. A huge mistake that caused us to lose the game.

In reality, it was not my fault but Xavier's, who had inadvertently fallen on me while I was throwing the ball.

This episode angered all the members of the team, and Michael, in a fit of anger, grabbed me by the arm and said:

"The handicapped should be on the bench!"

I don't like it when they call me handicapped or even when they touch me. So, on impulse, I punched him in the stomach. A lesson he would remember!

Dominique stood between us and, trying to calm me, invoked:

"Tobia, don't screw it up. Michael made a mistake, it's true, but you don't have to hit!"

"He-insulted-me!" I yelled angrily.

"You're right. But you don't have to hit anyway. Violence is not good for anyone!" he reiterated, raising his voice. Then, to change the subject, he told me about **Jerry Green**.

Jerry Green is my idol and plays for the Cantù basketball team, the most formidable team we have in Italy. It is the second best in Europe, after Real Madrid, and for this reason, it is called the Queen of Europe. I know everything about this team, but there is no need to recount the whole story. Then, Dominique pointed out to me that if I continued to train, I certainly could have performed better. Of course, I would never have become a Jerry Green, but I could have definitely become a good basketball player.

For the moment, I have not yet decided what I will do in life because I have other problems on my mind, such as, for example, seeing Pilù's jacket.

After that, we went to the classroom, the support class.

When we heard a knock, I was busy assembling a large puzzle.

The work had been ongoing for several days now because I couldn't find a crucial piece. So, I didn't raise my head but remained there, my neck bent and my messy hair falling over my eyes.

"Hello!" they said in chorus.

I pretended not to hear.

"We have come to apologize to you," Michael and Xavier said together, while Pilù, approaching me, asked me:

"Were you looking for this piece?"

I snatched it out of his hand furiously, then returned to the same position as before.

"Oh, Tobia," said Dominique, "your classmates are here; perhaps it is time to make peace."

I wasn't sure I wanted to make peace, but I turned around anyway. I looked at Michael, and I felt as if I were having a stroke. I was really confused because I never imagined I would see him again wearing the same clothes as before, with a jacket that was missing the first button.

Seeing my classmates again, my mind, like a movie camera, took me back several months.

We were with Mrs. Cristina's parrot. Michael wore a pair of green trousers and a green and brown checkered jacket. Then, he entered the cage and asked for water. When he came out with the glass in his hands, Mrs. Cristina's ring had disappeared, and he no longer had the first button of his jacket. In its place, a small hole accentuated the tear.

Seeing me so tense, Dominique said:

"Are you okay, Tobia?"

"I just found out something," I replied. Then, I pulled out the button and rocked it in front of Michael's eyes.

"Oh, thank you, Tobia," he said, taking it. Then, he added: "Finally, my button! Where did you find it?"

"Where you lost it!" interjected Dominique. "And that is in Mrs. Cristina's watch box. It was you who stole her ring; didn't you, Michael?" he said, completing his thought.

For a moment, there was absolute silence. I knew he was going to confess, so I felt my heart pounding in my chest. It was as if someone were turning the light on and off. My friend stood and looked at me with wide eyes, clearly surprised by what I had reserved for him. Xavier also looked at me, bewildered, as if he had been his accomplice. The only one who approached me, hugging me, was Pilù. Yes, he would never betray me; now I knew. I was so sorry that I had ever doubted him.

"W-H-Y?" I asked, finally.

Michael didn't breathe.

"Why?" I replied in a firm voice.

It was Xavier who answered:

When the carabinieri arrived, we were scared, so we thought about hiding the ring in your man purse. We would have gotten it back later, at the end of the search; but unfortunately, it didn't turn out that way.

Then I inhaled several times until my chest swelled like a turkey because I wanted to beat them. Afterward, as if nothing had happened, I took the last piece and stuck it in the only hole left, giving the landscape back its perfect outline.

The thieves would have been dealt with by the carabinieri, to whom I reported them. Meanwhile, I relished my moment of hard-earned triumph. Upon leaving school, I did something surprising: I treated myself to a large bouquet of mimosa, vibrant yellow like the sun, and buried my face in it. I enjoyed the gentle touch of its soft blooms and breathed in their fragrance: I felt innocent, just like the essence of the flower, and Pilù understood this.

Thanks to my friend, I reconciled with flowers. As if that weren't enough, I no longer wanted to be called handicapped because the mimosa, in its language, also meant freedom and autonomy!

A Mystery
to be Solved

Everything had ended brilliantly, and at school, in an act of apology, they celebrated. I was very happy because I had demonstrated that being a kleptomaniac does not necessarily mean being a thief. The carabinieri then congratulated me and called me the best budding policeman with special analytical skills in the square.

Those expressions were new to me, and a familiar black hole formed in my head. However, I didn't ask what 'budding policeman' and 'analytical faculties' meant because I was focused on enjoying the praise I received.

The biggest surprise was receiving a letter from Commissioner Lolita Lobosco, who also complimented me on how I had managed to identify the real thief.

That happiness, however, didn't last long because when I slipped under my bed to retrieve the box with my turtles, I found it uncovered.

Filled with anxiety, I glanced inside and noticed that Brilly was gone. Loly, however, was there munching on his lettuce before seeking refuge beneath the wood shavings in the housing I had constructed while at the Garden of Happy Children Center. In a panic, I then asked my family if they had seen my little turtle.

My father grumbled that he had other things to do besides running after my turtles. My brother Matthew sighed dramatically, then locked himself in his room because, "he had to study." My older brother

Hector, on the other hand, had been away from home for quite a while, so that was out of the question. The only suspect was my mother who, taken by a maniacal cleaning spree, was polishing the room with her vacuum cleaner and had certainly overturned the box.

"I'm sorry, Tobia. I promise to look for it as soon as I can!" she replied, breathless. Yet, I didn't want to hear logic; I was eager to find my Brilly immediately, so I objected:

My friend Pilù would have helped me look for her, if only I had permission to have him come to my house!

Mom sensed my nervousness, so in a conciliatory manner, she said:

"Please keep at bay those chicks that you sometimes hear scratching... Start looking for her yourself; surely she will be in a corner of the house! As soon as I can, I will help you. As for your friend Pier Luca... well, we'll see."

Like a truffle dog, I scoured under my bed, finally finding a piece of one of my puzzles that I had been searching for months. Between the skirting board and the foot of the bed base, I discovered the wheel of my red Ferrari and the ten of Clubs that Tommy had given me. Then, I headed to my brother's room. Like a snake, I slipped under his bed, where I found a little bit of everything: his stinky socks, a slipper and a mismatched shoe, and the detective stories The Murder of the Rue Saint-Roch and The Murders of the Rue Morgue (which my mother was looking for) along with a fifty-cent coin. I pocketed the coin and placed it in my man purse. Then, I removed my mismatched shoes and left the books by Edgar Allan Poe and Alexandre Dumas there, ensuring my mother continued to look for them in vain.

Under my brother Hector's bed, however, I found nothing at all; it was very clean. This made sense since he often lived away from home. As for my turtle, not even a shadow!

I dismantled my parents' room, rummaging through every little space; however, Brilly seemed to have melted away. Then it was time for the kitchen: I pulled out the bins for separated waste, the cart with all the cleaning supplies, the two-seater sofa, and the sideboard.

Finally, I entered the living room, where I flipped over the sofas, removed the carpet, and moved a small desk that served as a secretaire. I carefully inspected the plants, searched every corner of the house, and, in the end, I sat on the ground ready to give up.

It felt like a small revolution had taken place at home, as my father unleashed his frustrations on all the turtles in existence.

"Well, stop it!" he yelled. "It's not possible that a turtle, the size of a cheese wedge, can turn the house upside down!"

It was then that I experienced a nervous crisis. It felt like standing atop a mountain and watching the world revolve around me. I began to moan and breathe awkwardly until I turned red, while my mother tried in vain to calm me down:

"Calm down, Tobia; you'll see that, sooner or later, Brilly will pop up!"

I thought I needed to calm down and keep looking. I didn't have to give in to my crises, just as I didn't have to give in to anxiety. Therefore, I tried to reflect on what to do; however, my mind was so crowded with confusion that, in the end, I perceived it as an empty pumpkin.

Then I had an idea, and despite the chaos in my mind, I took Loly and placed her on the ground. If turtles in the wild feel the need to orient themselves to a specific place, my Loly had to find a direction. If I was lucky, my turtle would follow the same path as her companion Brilly, catching up with her.

I had forgotten to check the closet. Usually, that is a place with little traffic because it is where all the unused junk in the house is stored and where my parents typically keep several documents belonging to my family.

I ignored my mother's reproaches and, mimicking Chamomile, my aunt's cat, I followed Loly with a sly look as he took a precise direction. I saw him sneak into a corner of the shelf, and there he stayed. To see better, I took my pocket flashlight and directed the light into that hole: crouched one on top of the other were my two turtles. I screamed with happiness, but above all, I screamed because I had managed to find her: I had won. I reached in and grabbed them both, but a box full of documents fell at my feet.

To avoid further reproaches, I locked myself in the closet and tried to collect the files that had fallen. While I was gathering all those papers, I saw my name written on a letter that accompanied a series of photos and documents. Curious, I began to read:

REHABILITATION INSTITUTE
THE GARDEN OF HAPPY CHILDREN
HEALTH SERVICE CHARTER

Dear Mr. and Mrs. Barbato,

We are attaching the Health Service Charter along with some explanatory photos. This is intended as a gift for the children benefiting from rehabilitation at the Institute and their families, with the hope of ensuring a better quality of life for those in challenging situations.

This institute takes into account the needs of each individual, promoting the self-esteem and autonomy of the child.

The Center has sports fields, a carpentry workshop, leather oods, mechanics and ceramics, etc.

And more...

The Institute, in which you have placed your trust, will support the boy Tobia Barbato on the delicate path of growth. The seriousness and validity of the operators are guaranteed...

The letter continued with various other updates and concluded with a stamp and the Director's signature.

I looked at those papers again and felt confused. I couldn't be wrong; my name was right there on that letter. My parents wanted to take me back to the Institute, and I felt betrayed. Would my destiny be to live the rest of my life in an institute for the disabled, alone? I thought that I needed to solve that mystery as soon as possible, simply because I didn't want to go back to that place. My parents knew it, and they had even promised me. I had to prevent this from happening.

Worried, I placed Brilly and Loly back in the box, gave them some lettuce I had in my pocket, and lay down on the floor to think.

A Terrible
Misunderstanding

– CHAPTER 32 –

Then, I heard someone calling my name:

"Tobiaaa. Tobiaaa."

I thought it was my friend Tommy who was looking for me, or the educator, or Madame Fantasy.

Instead, it was my mother, who opened the closet door, exclaiming:

"Oh, Tobia, why don't you answer?"

The only noise that could be heard at that moment was the sound of Brilly and Loly scratching the bottom of the box with their carapaces while eating the salad.

"Have you found Brilly?" she asked. Then she added, "Please put your shoes back on."

"Mmh!" I muttered.

For a moment, I thought she was going to hit me because of the enormous mess I had created. Instead, she continued:

"What's going on here!? ... Oh, my God, what a revolution! It looks like a hurricane has passed through this closet!"

"It wasn't my fault!" I replied, showing her the turtles.

But she added, "What are all these papers?"

As she said this, she bent down, picking them up slowly. After each sheet that came into her hands, she kept on saying:

"Oh, my God, Tobia. Now I'll explain."

As she complained in that unbearable manner, attempting to provide an explanation, I found it hard to respond, even though the words were all in my head.

"Oh, my goodness, Tobia. Now I'll explain. It's not quite what you think!"

Then she stretched out her arms and tried to place the documents back on the shelf as best she could. When I looked up, I saw two large tears rolling down her cheeks, trickling onto the paper she was holding and creating a large stain of black ink.

It looked like one of those paintings that my teacher Giacomina imposed on me, with finger paints, when I was a child. I remember messing them up because black was a color I didn't like.

Then, she wiped her tears with the back of his hand. But her nose dripped, and she dabbed it with the cuff of her sweater. At last, clasping me to her breast, she said:

"No, Tobia. It's not as you think. It is a terrible misunderstanding. I could never, ever part with you."

Meanwhile, my father arrived, and together they tried to explain the origin of those papers to me. However, they could not make a coherent statement. They both spoke at the same time, creating a tremendous amount of confusion.

Suddenly, I thought I saw two people with a big problem. Their minds had gone haywire, just like it happens to me when I can't explain myself and I hear those little animals; that is, the chicks, wandering around in my head, making me say nonsense.

My mother said, "I told you to make that blessed letter disappear!" And my father answered, "It's not my fault that damn turtle decided to hide right there, in the closet, fuck!"

The story dragged on for a long time, with the two of them accusing each other. Finally, trying to exercise some self-control, my father said:

"Enough, we need clarification... Now I'll speak!"

While I waited for this clarification, I just looked at the hairs coming out of his nose and counted the holes that were on my mother's old sweater.

In the end, he managed to explain to me that the documents dated back to my previous stay at the Garden of Happy Children, so I didn't have to worry because they had no intention of bringing me back to the institute. From that day on, no one spoke of it anymore. I had to trust him, but I still wasn't at ease because, away from home, I would no longer see my brothers, as well as my father and mother...

A few weeks later, however, something else happened that I could never have imagined. I was sitting next to my brothers, finishing dinner and playing with the grains of rice floating in the broth. Listlessly, I avoided the parsley leaves and tomato fillets. My mother, on the other hand, exaggeratedly turned the spoon on the plate as she does when she is about to tell us something. I was starting to feel tired on that wooden chair when my father's voice stopped me.

"Listen..." he said, his mouth full of soup. "I've got something important to share that your mother and I have been discussing. We've given it considerable thought and genuinely believe we're making the right choice. We're planning to help a family, or more specifically, a boy. We've considered asking for that boy in foster care; it's a form of adoption..."

He swallowed, wiped his mouth with a napkin, and after taking another spoonful, he added, "For you, it will feel like gaining another brother. Our lives will be enriched by his presence. He'll visit us whenever he likes. Now, don't look at me that way; it's a surprise... If I revealed who he is, it wouldn't be a surprise anymore!"

I looked at him, confused. He barely resembled the dad I knew. What he had just said was news that sent a tingling sensation through my chest, gradually spreading throughout my body. It felt as if something first moved toward my stomach and then up to my throat. It was as though many hearts were beating together in my chest.

"Damn," I thought, "it's another *Thriller* to solve!"

Four Brothers

So another brother was about to arrive. In my own way, I organized my thoughts.

"Tobia is a boy:

With two parents who love him.

With two brothers who love him.

With a new brother he is about to meet."

Then I remembered that the teacher Giacomina always corrected me when I wrote in the third person, so I corrected:

"**I am** a boy:

With two parents who love me.

With two brothers who love me.

With a new brother I am about to meet."

I went to bed, but I couldn't sleep. All those changes in such a short time! I got up late at night and left the house, positioning myself on the street toward the garage where my father's car was parked; I wanted to think.

I sat on the sidewalk, wearing my plush pajamas, and stayed there until I saw the sun rise in the sky, accompanied by certain blurred flashes.

I wondered what this new brother would be like. Would he listen to my bizarre speeches? Would he play with me? But above all, would he love me?

I stopped thinking when I heard my parents' voices calling for me anxiously. A total of four hours and six minutes had passed. They were even numbers, and this gave me comfort.

"Did you want to run away again?" my father expressed, taking me back into the house.

But I didn't answer. I wanted to tell him that, deep down, I was afraid they would lock me up again in the institute. Instead, I just smiled, simply because I'm not good at making difficult speeches. However, a few words were on the tip of my tongue that I really needed to say to her:

"Do you love me?"

"Of course, Tobia, what questions are you asking us? You know very well that we love you. We all love you!"

"I know. But I want to understand..." Then I added, "I love you too. I'm improving a lot. I have changed, I am no longer the usual Tobia who makes a fuss, who is rigid and throws tantrums. Did you see? I'm just getting better!"

"Thank you," they said, wiping their eyes.

Recently, they found it easy to cry. You couldn't mention them starting to cry, and, with the excuse of a cold, they went to the bathroom to wipe away their tears.

"Thank you for what?" I asked.

"Because you love us and because you say so many beautiful things!" Then Mother led me back to bed and begged me to sleep a little.

One morning, I had just finished giving a lettuce leaf to Brilly and Loly when Mother approached me and said:

"Tobia, your father and I have a surprise for you. However, be patient once again, please!"

"I don't like surprises, you know," I said.

"Of course I know. But this is different..." she answered, caressing me.

I didn't escape, but I made a sound that closely resembled a lament. Then, to keep myself occupied, I took the Rubik's magic cube, which my father had given me, from the drawer and began aligning the red color on the same side.

The solution is obtained in layers and is also called "layer by layer." It consists of solving the three layers of the cube in succession: upper, middle, and lower. This is achieved through an internal mechanism that allows the rotation of the planes in every direction.

"Can you hear me, Tobia?" she insisted.

Unfazed, I kept manipulating the cube. I had completed the first side and was getting ready to reassemble the second.

"Tobia, soon your new brother will be here..." she continued, timidly.

"Is this the surprise?" I said, concentrating on putting the green back together.

"There's more..." she answered.

Once, the teacher Giacomina told me that life is also made up of surprises, which can be good or bad. When surprises are bad, you feel bad. That's why I didn't like them: there's always the risk that they could disappoint you. Then, I thought there would be four of us with the other new brother. Yes, four brothers; I didn't mind it at all. I paused to think for a while. The number four is an even number, and that is a good thing. Furthermore, not taking risks in life means losing from the start.

It took me over ten minutes to complete the magic cube. If I wanted to beat the world record, which belongs to Erik Akkersdijk, I still needed to practice a lot to reach the 7.08 minutes from July 2008.

On the other hand, my parents spent the whole evening giving me the most amazing surprise of my life. Yes, my new brother was none other than my friend Pier Luca.

I stood there with my mouth open, trying to understand. But hadn't my father always been distrustful of my friend? Turning to him, I said:

"Have you changed your mind about Pilù?"

"You know, sometimes in life, you make a mistake in judging people, and your mother and I want to make amends."

If what they were telling me was true, then it meant that I had to start recording the news in my brain.

I had to start seeing him more as a brother than as a friend. But what amazed me most was the fact that I had always felt him close as a brother in my heart.

"So, what do you think?" Mom said, red in the face.

"Hmm..." I was speechless.

"So?" she urged me again.

It occurred to me to thank her for what she and my father had done, but I didn't have the right words, so I remained silent. Then I remembered Dominique's suggestion to "Say it with flowers," and I decided it was time to follow his advice.

My family truly loved me, fulfilling a wish I had never had the courage to express. Finally, I realized that I loved life; I had always loved it. I had clung to it since my first cry. That morning, I filled the house with strawberry trees, farmhouses, gerberas, and red tulips. I wanted them to know that I loved only them, that I felt gratitude for what they had done, that there was so much joy in our home, and that my love was sincere.

I was eager to give meaning to my life!

Now, I wanted to learn how to gaze at the stars and the moon with its pale glow. I wanted to run freely in the meadows and gather all the flowers in the world. I wanted to watch the sun travel across the sky from east to west. I wanted to feel the rain on my skin and let the wind embrace me. I wanted to understand why wheat, from soft green grass, ripens under the summer sun and then sprouts again.

I was happy. Just like that time my father shaved me and said:

"Tobia, you have grown up!"

I looked at my parents then and felt that I loved them very much.

P.S. I can't close my story without writing to my teacher, Giacomina. So, with Pilù, I turned on the computer that dominates my room and started...

Letters and Recipes

— CHAPTER 34 —

Date 20/6/20013 13:30
From: "Tobia Barbato" <tobiabarbato84@libero.it>
To: "Giacomina Lamarna" <giacomilamarna@libero.it>
Subject: FunThriller
Attachments: letter from Tobia

Dear Teacher Giacomina,

I am writing this letter to you on the computer while thinking of you. My mother, like Tommy, told me that correspondence written and sent through the computer is called Mail, but I don't understand foreign words, so I continue to call it a letter.

I am writing to inform you that school has ended. This has been a very stressful year because I have learned to use the computer and study all the other subjects independently. At school, there is Dominique, who is obsessed with flowers and even claims that I am now grown up, so I have to behave like an adult. But I already act grown up; it's the adults who don't.

141

Now I'm at home with my mom, who has assigned me a task with a difficult title to keep me busy: "Write a letter to your best friend."

I only had Pilù as a friend, but he has now become my third brother. As a result, I no longer have male friends, so I changed the title to: "Write a letter to your best female friend."

So, the letter I wanted to write to you, which has been on my mind for some time, is now also homework.

Dear Teacher Giacomina, since you left, I have "come to terms with your absence." I have only just understood these words, which are my father's. They indicate that I have grown up and, in life, I must fend for myself.

I believe that I can do it because next year I will be in my third year of high school.

The professors say that I truly deserved this promotion. My special needs teacher, Dominique, mentioned that I am a smart guy because I solved a very intricate mystery.

I asked him what "intricate" means, and he replied that it means "difficult." He also told me that I'm a good guy, a budding cop with excellent analytical skills, just as the carabinieri had defined me.

But adults sometimes use different language, so I finally asked him what "budding policeman with analytical faculties" means. He laughed a lot and then explained to me that it refers to those people who possess intuition and are passionate about creative activities. Since I am a very intuitive guy, I named this new recreational activity of mine "FunThriller," which turned out to be not so recreational after all. In fact, my reputation has suffered because of kleptomania, the disorder I am trying to cure.

The theft of the ring has now been solved, and I am very happy because I have been found innocent.

There's one more thing you need to know. My parents will no longer take me to the Institute, and to make me happy, they have also asked for the custody of my friend Pilù, which is a kind of adoption, allowing him to come to my house whenever he wants. So now, there are six of us. It's an even number, and this makes me calm.

My mother, quoting a phrase by a certain François Rabelais, always tells me:

"You know, Tobia, a boy is not a vase to be filled, but a fire to be lit." I didn't understand very well what it meant, but I feel that she dedicates herself to me with a lot of love.

Now, I don't know what I'm going to do when I grow up. I'd like to be a mechanic or maybe a "budding cop," as Dominique puts it.

I could travel to Australia with my brother Pilù to hunt parrots, but without that old trout, Mrs. Cristina.

And do you know that I fell in love? Maybe I'll marry that pullet of my classmate Maria, as Pilù calls her, because when I see her, I always get a blow to my heart.

What do you say, will I succeed?

And with this letter, or rather, email, I conclude my album that you helped me begin some time ago regarding the whole issue of the theft.

Well, now I'm truly done. But I want to express that I miss you a great deal, and I also miss your sweets. Mom says that when we love people, they stay inside us forever.

Here is a letter to my best friend.

I love you,
Tobia

P.S. Do you remember those strange chicks? Well, every now and then they still appear in my head, but I try to fight them... My turtles, on the other hand, are fine. I no longer suck my thumb, and I have learned to love flowers too.

Date: 21/6/2013 14:00
From: "Giacomina Lamarna" giacomilamarna@libero.it
To: "Tobia Barbato" tobiabarbato@libero.it
Subject: FunThriller
Attachment: letter from teacher Giacomina

Dear Tobia,

After lunch, I opened my email and, to my surprise, found your email or, if we really want to be picky, your letter!

Apparently, Mom's "assignment" has served not only to make you practice on the computer but also to entice you to write to me!

Ever since I first met you when you were very young, I have believed in your abilities. You are a smart guy, and I am very proud of both your academic achievements and your outstanding work as a budding cop with great analytical skills, just to use the definition of the carabinieri and your professor Dominique.

Your intelligence—and, let me add, your infuriating stubbornness—helped you uncover the real culprit behind the theft of Mrs. Cristina's ring. Rightly so, your pride, but above all your innocence, was at stake, in addition to your tendency to take possession of everything you like, which is known as kleptomania.

I have never doubted your honesty and abilities, and I am confident you will succeed in life. I like the definition "FunThriller"; you will see that it will bring you luck.

This reinforces my belief: there are no handicapped people, only individuals with different abilities. I, for example, could never have done what you did in coining that nice definition to describe a detective story. However, I managed to prepare the fruit cakes that you enjoy so much.

You know, Tobia, I also feel nostalgic for all the afternoons we spent together; we had such a great time. However, life changes, and my new job as a permanent teacher forced me to make a choice. That's why your dad told you to get over it.

It was right for you to grow up and get used to my absence. Now, you have Dominique, who will help you finish your high school studies, and since he was involved in the investigation, I believe he is also quite intelligent.

You shared something important about your life. Your parents have requested custody of your friend Pier Luca. Let me tell you, having "adopted" your friend is so beautiful that there are no words to define this gesture of love.

Very beautiful, and the quote from your mother is touching! Tobia, that certain François Rabelais, a French humanist, speaks the truth when he says that a boy is not a vase to be filled, but a fire to be lit. Children, my dear, must be educated for life, but they also need the freedom to express their personalities, which should be nurtured just like the flowers you have learned to love! And remember, life is a mystery worth discovering. I'm sure you will embrace it!

It's wonderful that you're in love, dear Tobia. Keep in mind that love is a unique, spontaneous, and generous feeling.

And then, I must share a secret: you and your family taught me how to love! It's a lesson I'll never forget. Because of this and so much more, you will always hold a special place in my heart.

I will read your story, and I recommend... Neve give up.

I love you too.
Your teacher, Giacomina

P.S. Blessed chicks... Hold on, you will see that sooner or later, they will leave you alone. The fact that you no longer suck your thumb is a significant milestone: you have definitely grown up.

As for the flowers, it means you will be the flower who remains in my heart forever!

From Tobia's red notebook:

ORANGE CARPACCIO

Ingredients for two people:
(2) Large juicy oranges
Black pepper
Brandy to taste
(2) Tablespoons of brown sugar
*pearl brown sugar orange blossoms (wash the flowers in the brandy, then roll them in the brown sugar sprinkles).

Preparation:
Peel the oranges, taking care to free them from the white skin and cut them into many large slices. In a flat dish, place the orange blossoms pearled with brown sugar, placing the juicy slices on top, previously sprinkled with brandy and with sugar; sprinkle everything with black pepper.

CHICKEN SCALLOPS WITH ORANGE

Ingredients for two people:
(4) Slices of chicken breasts
(2) Large oranges, salt
Half a cup of oil
Durum wheat flour (to taste)
A tablespoon of sultanas
A splash of brandy
*red rose petals sprinkled with brandy.

Preparation:
Cut the chicken breasts into many medallions and flour them.
Heat the oil in a non-stick pan and place the medallions on it.
After browning them, salt and add the orange juice, cooking
them gently, making sure that everything remains creamy and
soft. A few minutes before turning off, add the sultanas and
a splash of brandy. Cover and serve warm on a bed of red
rose petals.

ORANGE MARMALADE

Ingredients:
(4) Large juicy oranges
(2) Fresh lemons
A cup of sugar
Half a cup of brandy or rum
A pinch of cinnamon
Water to taste.
*orange blossom, a handful.

Preparation:
Peel the oranges and cut them into cubes, taking care to remove
the seeds. Wash only one of the peels well, remove and discard
the white part, and chop it. Wash the lemons and cut them into
wedges, removing the seeds. Place everything in a pot with a
little water, then cook gently. When the mixture is soft and ho-
mogeneous, add the sugar. Cook over low heat for the necessary
time, taking care that the contents do not dry out too much.
Finally, add a pinch of cinnamon, brandy or rum, and a handful
of orange blossom.
Sterilize the jars, then pour in the boiling jam and seal. Put the
jars to sleep for twelve hours in a woolen blanket.

FROZEN ORANGE SKEWERS

Ingredients:
(2) Juicy oranges,
Brown sugar
Rum
(4) Long toothpicks
Aluminum foil, just enough.
*yellow and red rosebuds washed in rum and rolled in brown sugar.

Preparation:
Peel the orange, also removing the white part, without affecting the film that wraps the wedges. Divide it into wedges, possibly of two. The lunettes obtained are first soaked in rum and dipped in brown sugar, then pierced with toothpicks alternately with the rose buds, and wrapped in foil. Place the skewers in the freezer before consuming them in drinks of your liking.